Forrest Carter, whose Indian name is Little Tree, is the author of "Gone To Texas," published last year and made into a movie by Warner Brothers under the title "The Outlaw Josey Wales." In a sequel, "The Vengeance Trail of Josey Wales" (Delacorte, $6.95) Josey heads into Mexico after reneg a de Gen- eral Escobedo, but this new western is m a lfted by violence and gunplay in spite of its fair trea tment of the Apache to whom the new book is dedi c ated.

Third World?

they take the credit."

He shuts his eyes for a few seconds then resumes, "What hurt me deeply, though, was when my people did not understand my music."

Taj commiserates briefly over the fact many blacks view his music with contempt — like it's an obscene glimpse back to plantation slavery and peanut patches. And he acknowledges many blacks have cast behind his music in favor of another, one that too often emulates flashy, gun-toting flesh dealers pushing around town in leopard skin El Dorados with a heart cut out in the back window.

"But they can't forget their past," he asserts in his raspy voice. "It's ridiculous for them to ignore their roots. If my name was Carlos Santiago and I was Mexican, I could do folk songs for my people and they'd be proud. But when it came to doing the same thing for my people, it wasn't their rejection alone. I have found the record companies have strangled us. They said then

'Don't move ahead, don't move sideways.'

"They created a culture, a bunch of people and a deadend out of mediocrity. And that," he raps his massive knuckles sharply against the table, "is how we're manipulated. You never know what you should know and they only tell you about what you don't need."

He sighs finally, "You can carry a little knowledge and travel fine but ignorance around your neck keeps you under someone's foot."

GOREN

**BY CHARLES H. GOREN
AND OMAR SHARIF**

© 1976, The Chicago Tribune

DEAR MR. GOREN

Q. — I thought that all n trump bids promise balanced distribution. In game last night I held th following: ♠ 93 ♡ 8 ◇ AJ4 ♣ Q87543. Partner opene the bidding one heart, I r sponded two clubs and

Gone to Texas

GONE TO TEXAS

FORREST CARTER

DELACORTE PRESS/ELEANOR FRIEDE

Designed by Ann Spinelli

Library of Congress Cataloging in Publication Data

Carter, Forrest.
Gone to Texas.

First published in 1973 under title: The rebel outlaw,
Josey Wales.
I. Title.

PZ4.C3235Go3   [PS3553.A777]   813'.5'4   74–23172

ISBN: 0–440–04565–7

For Ten Bears

Preface

Missouri is called the "Mother of Outlaws." She acquired her title in the aftermath of the Civil War, when bitter men who had fought without benefit of rules in the Border War (a war within a War) could find no place for themselves in a society of old enmities and Reconstruction government. They rode and lived aimlessly, in the vicious circle of reprisal, robbery, and shoot-out that led to nowhere. The Cause was gone, and all that remained was personal feud, retribution . . . and survival. Many of them drifted to Texas.

If Missouri was the Mother, then Texas was the Father . . . the refuge, with boundless terrain and bloody frontier, where a proficient pistolman could find reason for existence and room to ride. The initials

"GTT," hurriedly carved on the doorpost of a Southern shack, was message enough to relatives and friends that the carver was in "law trouble," and Gone To Texas.

In those days they weren't called "gunfighters"; that came in the 1880's from the dime noveleers. They were called "pistolmen," and they referred to their weapon as a "pistol," or by the make . . . a "Colts' .44." The Missouri guerrilla was the first expert pistolman. According to U.S. Army dispatches, the guerrillas used this "new" war weapon with devastating results.

This is the story of one of those outlaws.

The outlaws . . . and the Indians . . . are real . . . they lived; lived in a time when the meaning of "good" or "bad" depended mostly on the jasper who was saying it. There were too many wrongs mixed in with what we thought were the "rights"; so we shall not try to judge them here . . . but simply, to the best of our ability, to "tell it like it is" . . . or was.

The men . . . white and red . . . and the times that produced them . . . and how they lived it out . . . to finish the course.

PART 1

1

The dispatch was filed December 8, 1866:

FROM: Central Missouri Military District. Major
      Thomas Bacon, 8th Kansas Cavalry, Com-
      manding.

TO: Headquarters, Texas Military District, Galves-
      ton, Texas. Major General Charles Griffin,
      Commanding.

Dispatch filed with: General Philip Sheridan, South-
      west Military District, New Orleans, Louisi-
      ana.

DAYLIGHT ROBBERY OF MITCHELL BANK, LEXINGTON,
LAFAYETTE COUNTY, MISSOURI DECEMBER 4 THIS IN-
STANT. BANDITS ESCAPING WITH EIGHT THOUSAND DOL-
LARS, U.S. ARMY PAYROLL: NEW-MINTED TWENTY-
DOLLAR GOLD PIECES. PURSUIT TOWARD INDIAN

NATIONS TERRITORY. BELIEVED HEADED SOUTH TO
TEXAS. ONE BANDIT SEVERELY WOUNDED. ONE IDENTI-
FIED. DESCRIPTION FOLLOWS:
JOSEY WALES, AGE 32. 5 FEET 9 INCHES. WEIGHT 160
POUNDS. BLACK EYES, BROWN HAIR, MEDIUM MUS-
TACHE. HEAVY BULLET SCAR HORIZONTAL RIGHT CHEEK-
BONE, DEEP KNIFE SCAR LEFT CORNER MOUTH. PREVI-
OUSLY LISTED WANTED BY U.S. MILITARY AS EX-
GUERRILLA LIEUTENANT SERVING WITH CAPT. WILLIAM
"BLOODY BILL" ANDERSON. WALES REFUSED AMNESTY-
SURRENDER, 1865. IN ADDITION TO CRIMINAL ACTIVITY,
MUST BE REGARDED AS INSURRECTIONIST REBEL.
ARMED AND DANGEROUS. THREE-THOUSAND-DOLLAR RE-
WARD OFFERED BY U.S. MILITARY, MISSOURI DISTRICT.
DEAD OR ALIVE.

It was cold. The wind whipped the wet pines into
mournful sighing and sped the rain like bullets. It
caused the campfires to jump and flicker and the soldiers around them to curse commanding officers and
the mothers who gave them birth.

The campfires were arranged in a curious half-
moon, forming a flickering chain that closed about
these foothills of the Ozark Mountains. In the dark,
cloud-scudding night the bright dots looked like a net
determined to hold back the mountains from advanc-
ing into the Neosho River Basin, Indian Nations, just
beyond.

Josey Wales knew the meaning of the net. He squatted, two hundred yards back in the hollow of heavy
pine growth, and watched . . . and chewed with slow
contemplation at a wad of tobacco. In nearly eight
years of riding, how many times had he seen the cir-
cle-net of Yankee Cavalry thrown out around him?

It seemed a hundred years ago, that day in 1858. A

young farmer, Josey Wales, following the heavy turning plow in the creek bottoms of Cass County, Missouri. It would be a two-mule crop this year, a big undertaking for a mountain man, and Josey Wales was mountain. ALL the way back through his great-grandfolk of the past in the blue ridges of Virginia; the looming, smoke-haze peaks of Tennessee and into the broken beauty of the Ozarks; always it had been the mountains. The mountains were a way of life; independence and sanctuary, a philosophy that lent the peculiar code to the mountain man. "Where the soil's thin, the blood's thick," was their clannishness. To rectify a wrong carried the same obligation as being beholden to a favor. It was a religion that went beyond thought but rather was marrowed in the bone that lived or died with the man.

Josey Wales, with his young wife and baby boy, had come to Cass County. That first year he "obligated" himself for forty acres of flatland. He had built the house with his own hands and raised a crop . . . and now this year he had obligated for forty more acres that took in the creek bottom. Josey Wales was "gittin' ahead." He hitched his mules to the turning plow in the dark of morning and waited in the fields, rested on his plow stock, for the first dim light that would allow him to plow.

It was a long time before Josey saw the smoke rising, that spring morning of 1858. The creek bottom was new ground, and the plow jerked at the roots, and Josey had to gee-haw the mules around the stumps. He hadn't looked up until he heard the shots. It was then he saw the smoke. It rose black-gray over the ridge. It could only be the house. He had left the mules, running barefoot, overalls flapping against his skinny legs; wildly, through the briars and sumac, across the rocky gullies. There had been little left when he fell, exhausted, into the swept clearing. The timbers of the cabin had fallen in. The fire was a guttering smoke that had already filled its appetite. He ran, fell, ran again . . . around and around the ruin, screaming his wife's name, calling the baby boy, until his voice hoarsened into a whisper.

He had found them there in what had been the kitchen. They had fallen near the door, and the blackened skeleton arms of the baby boy were clinging to his mother's neck. Numbly, mechanically, Josey had gotten two sacks from the barn and rolled up the charred figures in them. He dug their single grave beneath the big water oak at the edge of the yard, and as darkness fell and moonlight silvered over the ruins, he tried to render the Christian burial.

But his Bible remembering would only come in snatches. "Ashes to ashes . . . dust to dust," he had mumbled through his blackened face. "The Lord gives and the Lord takes away." "Ye're fer me 'er agin' me, said Jesus." And finally, "An eye fer an eye . . . a tooth fer a tooth."

Great tears rolled down the smoked face of Josey Wales there in the moonlight. A tremble shook his body with uncontrollable fierceness that chattered his teeth and jerked his head. It was the last time Josey Wales would cry.

2

Though raiding had taken place back and forth across the Missouri-Kansas Border since 1855, the burning of Josey Wales' cabin was the first of the Kansas "Redleg" raids to hit Cass County. The names of Jim Lane, Doc Jennison, and James Montgomery were already becoming infamous as they led looting armies of pillagers into Missouri. Beneath a thinly disguised "cause" they set the Border aflame.

Josey Wales had "taken to the brush," and there he found others. They were guerrilla veterans, these young farmers, by the time the War between the States began. The formalities of governments in conflict only meant an occupying army that drove them deeper into the brush. They already had their War. It was not a formal conflict with rules and courtesy, bat-

tles that began and ended . . . and rest behind the
lines. There were no lines. There were no rules. Theirs
was a war to the knife, of burned barn and ravaged
countryside, of looted home and outraged womenfolk.
It was a blood feud. The Black Flag became a flag of
honorable warning: "We ask no quarter, we give
none." And they didn't.

When Union General Ewing issued General Order
Eleven to arrest the womenfolk, to burn the homes, to
depopulate the Missouri counties along the Border of
Kansas, the guerrilla ranks swelled with more riders.
Quantrill, Bloody Bill Anderson, whose sister was
killed in a Union prison, George Todd, Dave Pool,
Fletcher Taylor, Josey Wales; the names grew in in-
famy in Kansas and Union territory, but they were the
"boys" to the folks.

Union raiders launching the infamous "Night of
Blood" in Clay County bombed a farmhouse that tore
off the arm of a mother, killed her young son, and sent
two more sons to the ranks of the guerrillas. They
were Frank and Jesse James.

Revolvers were their weapons. They were the first to
perfect pistol work. With reins in teeth, a Colts' pistol
in each hand, their charges were a fury in suicidal
mania. Where they struck became names in bloody
history. Lawrence, Centralia, Fayette, and Pea Ridge.
In 1862 Union General Halleck issued General Order
Two: "Exterminate the guerrillas of Missouri; shoot
them down like animals, hang all prisoners." And so it
was like animals they became, hunted, turning
viciously to strike their adversaries when it was to their
advantage. Jennison's Redlegs sacked and burned Day-
ton, Missouri, and the "boys" retaliated by burning
Aubry, Kansas, to the ground, fighting Union patrols
all the way back to the Missouri mountains. They slept

in their saddles or rolled up under bushes with reins in their hands. With muffled horses' hooves, they would slip through Union lines to cross the Indian Nations on their way to Texas to lick their wounds and regroup. But always they came back.

As the tide of the Confederacy ebbed toward defeat, the blue uniforms multiplied along the Border. The ranks of the "boys" began to thin. On October 26, 1864, Bloody Bill died with two smoking pistols in his hands. Hop Wood, George Todd, Noah Webster, Frank Shepard, Bill Quantrill . . . the list grew longer . . . the ranks thinner. The peace was signed at Appomattox, and word began to filter into the brush that amnesty-pardons were to be granted to the guerrillas. It was little Dave Pool who had brought the word to eighty-two of the hardened riders. Around the campfire of an Ozark mountain hollow he explained it to them that spring evening.

"All a feller has to do is ride in to the Union post, raise his right hand, and swear sich as he'll be loyal to the United States. Then," said Dave, "he kin taken up his hoss . . . and go home."

Boots scuffed the ground, but the men said nothing. Josey Wales, his big hat pulled low to his eyes, squatted back from the fire. He still held the reins of his horse . . . as if he had only paused here for the moment. Dave Pool kicked a pine knot into the fire, and it popped and skittered with smoke.

"Guess I'll be ridin' in, boys," he said quietly and moved to his horse. Almost as one the men rose and walked to their horses. They were a savage-looking crew. The heavy pistols sagged in holsters from their waists. Some of them wore shoulder pistols as well, and here and there long knives at their belts picked up a twinkle from the campfire. They had been accused of many things, of most of which they were guilty, but cowardice was not one of them. As they swung to their mounts they looked back across the campfire and saw the lone figure still squatting. The horses stomped impatiently, but the riders held them. Pool advanced his horse toward the fire.

"Air ye' goin', Josey?" he asked.

There was a long silence. Josey Wales did not lift his eyes from the fire. "I reckin not," he said.

Dave Pool turned his horse. "Good luck, Josey," he called and lifted his hand in half salute.

Other hands were lifted, and the calls of " 'Luck" drifted back . . . and they were gone.

All except one. After a long moment the rider slowly walked his horse into the circle of firelight. Young Jamie Burns stepped from his mount and looked across the fire at Josey. "Why, Josey? Why don't ye go?"

Josey looked at the boy. Eighteen years old, rail-thin, with hollowed cheeks and blond hair that spilled to his shoulders beneath the slouch hat. "Ye'd best make haste and ketch up with 'em, boy," Josey said, almost tenderly. "A lone rider won't never make it."

The boy smoothed the ground with a toe of his heavy boot. "I've rid with ye near 'bout two year now, Josey . . ." he paused, "I was . . . jest wonderin' why."

Josey stood and walked to the fire, leading his horse. He gazed intently into the flames. "Well," he said quietly, "I jest cain't . . . anyhow, there ain't nowheres to go."

If Josey Wales had understood all the reasons, which he did not, he still could not have explained them to the boy. There was, in truth, no place for Josey Wales to go. The fierce mountain clan code would have deemed it a sin for him to take up life. His loyalty was there, in the grave with his wife and baby. His obligation was to the feud. And despite the cool cunning he had learned, the animal quickness and the deliberate arts of killing with pistol and knife, beneath it all there still rose the black rage of the mountain man. His family had been wronged. His wife and boy murdered. No people, no government, no king, could ever repay. He did not think these thoughts. He only felt the feeling of generations of the code handed down from the Welsh and Scot clans and burned into his being. If there was nowhere to go, it did not mean emptiness in the life of Josey Wales. That emptiness was filled with a cold hatred and a bitterness that showed when his black eyes turned mean.

Jamie Burns sat down on a log. "I ain't got nowheres to go neither," he said.

A mockingbird suddenly set up song from a honeysuckle vine. A wood thrush chuckled for night nesting.

"Have ye got a chaw?" Jamie asked.

Josey pulled a green-black twist from his pocket and handed it across the fire. The man and the boy were partners.

3

Josey Wales and Jamie Burns "took to the brush." The following month Jesse James tried to surrender under a flag of truce and was shot through the lungs, barely escaping. When the news reached Josey his opinion of the enemy's treachery was reinforced, and he smiled coldly as he gave Jamie the news, "I could've told little Dingus,*" he said.

There were others like them. In February, 1866, Josey and Jamie joined Bud and Donnie Pence, Jim Wilkerson, Frank Gregg, and Oliver Shephard in a daylight robbery of the Clay County Savings Bank at Liberty. Outlawry exploded over Missouri. A Missouri Pacific train was held up at Otterville. Federal Troops were reinforced, and the Governor ordered out militia and cavalry.

* "Dingus" was the nickname given Jesse James by his comrades.

But now the old haunts were gone. Twice they barely escaped capture or death through betrayal. The riding was growing more treacherous. They began to talk of Texas. Josey had ridden the trail five times, but Jamie had never. As fall brought its golden haze of melancholy to the Ozarks and the hint of cold wind from the north, Josey announced to the boy over a morning campfire, "After Lexington we're goin' to Texas." The bank at Lexington was a legitimate "target" for guerrillas. "Carpetbag bank, Yank Army payroll," Josey said. But they had gone against the rules, without a third man outside of the bank.

Jamie, with his flat gray eyes, coolly manned the door while Josey took the payroll. They had hit, guerrilla-style, bold and open, in the afternoon. When they came out, jerking the slipknot of their reins from the hitch rack, it was Jamie first up and riding his little mare. As Josey jerked his reins loose he had dropped the money bag, and as he stooped to retrieve it the reins had slipped from his hand. At that moment a shot rang out from the bank. The big roan had bolted, and Josey, instead of chasing the horse, had crouched, the money bag at his feet, and with a Colts' .44 in each hand poured a staccato roar of gunfire at the bank. He would have died there, for his instinct was not that of the criminal to run and save his loot, but that of the guerrilla, to turn on his hated enemies.

As people crowded out of the stores and blue uniforms poured out of the courthouse, Jamie whirled his horse and drummed back up the street, the little mare stretching out. He grabbed the trailing reins of the roan and while Josey turned the big .44's toward the scattering crowd he calmly led the roan at a canter back to the lone figure in the street.

Josey had holstered his pistols, grabbed up the bag,

and swung on the horse Indian-fashion as it broke into a dead run. Down the street they had come, the horses side by side, straight at the blue uniforms. The soldiers scattered, but as the horses came near to a scope of woods just ahead, the soldiers, kneeling, opened up with carbines. Josey heard the hard splat of the bullet and brought the big roan close to Jamie . . . or the boy would have fallen from the saddle.

Josey slowed the horses, holding the arm of Jamie as they came down into the brakes of the Missouri River. Turning northeast along the river, Josey brought the horses to a walk in the heavy willow growth and finally halted them. Far off in the distance he could hear men shouting back and forth as they worked their way into the brakes.

Jamie Burns had been hit hard. Josey swung down from his horse and lifted the jacket of the boy. The heavy rifle slug had entered his back, just missing the spine, but had emerged through his lower chest. Dark blood was caked over his trousers and saddle, and lighter blood still spurted from his wound. Jamie gripped the saddle horn with both hands.

"It's right bad, ain't it, Josey?" he asked with surprising calm.

Josey's answer was a quick nod as he pulled two shirts from Jamie's saddlebags and tore them into strips. He worked quickly making heavy pads and placed them on the open wounds, front and back, and then wound the stripping tightly around the boy. As Josey finished his work Jamie looked down at him from beneath the old slouch hat.

"I ain't gittin' off this hoss, Josey. I kin make it. Me and you seen fellers in lot worse shape make it, ain't we, Josey?"

Josey rested his hand over the tightly gripped hands

of the boy. He made the gesture in a rough, careless way . . . but Jamie felt the meaning. "Thet we have, Jamie," Josey looked steadily up at him, "and we'll make it by a long-tailed mile."

The sounds of horses breaking willows made Josey swing up on his horse. He turned in his saddle and said quietly to Jamie, "Jest hold on and let thet little mare follow me."

"Where to?" Jamie whispered.

A rare smile crossed the scarred face of the outlaw.

"Why, we're goin' where all good brush fighters go . . . where we ain't expected," he drawled. "We're doubling back to Lexington, nat'uly."

The dusk of evening was bringing on a quick darkness as they came out of the brakes. Josey set their course a few hundred yards north of the trail they had taken out of town, but angling so that it appeared they were headed for Lexington, though their direction would take them slightly north of the settlement. He never broke the horses into a trot but kept them walking steadily. The sounds of the shouting men on the river bank grew fainter and were finally lost behind them.

Josey knew the posse of militia and cavalry were searching for their crossing of the Missouri River. He pulled his horse back alongside the mare. Jamie's mouth was set in a grim line of pain, but he appeared steady in the saddle.

"Thet posse figures us fer Clay County," Josey said, "where little Dingus and Frank is stompin' around at."

Jamie tried to speak, but a quick jolt of pain cut his breath into a half shriek. He nodded his head that he understood.

As they rode, Josey reloaded the Colts and checked

the loads of the two pistols in his saddle holsters. With quick glances over his shoulder, he betrayed his anxiety for Jamie. Once, with the icy calm of the seasoned guerrilla, he held the horses on a wooded knoll while a score of possemen galloped past on their way to the river. Even as the horses thundered close, not fifty yards from their concealment, Josey was down off his mount and checking the bandages under Jamie's shirt.

"Look down at me, boy," he said. "Iff'n you look at 'em they might git a feelin'."

There was dried blood on the tight bandages, and Josey grunted with satisfaction. "We're in good shape, Jamie. The bleeding has stopped."

Josey swung aboard the roan and clucked the horses forward. He turned in the saddle to Jamie, "We'll jest keep walkin' 'til we walk slap out of Missouri."

The lights of Lexington showed on their right and then slowly receded behind them. West of Lexington there were Kansas City and Fort Leavenworth with a large contingent of soldiers; Richmond was north with a cavalry detachment of Missouri Militia; to the east were Fayette and Glasgow with more cavalry. Josey turned the horses south. All the way to the Blackwater River there was nothing except scattered farms. True, Warrensburg was just across the river, but first they had to put miles between themselves and Lexington.

Boldly, Josey turned onto the Warrensburg road. He pulled the mare up beside him, for he knew that Jamie was weakening and he feared the boy would fall from his horse. The hours and miles fell behind them. The road, though dangerous to travel, presented no obstacles to the horses, and the tough animals were accustomed to long forced marches.

As the first gray light streaked the clouds to the east, Josey jerked the horses to a standstill. For a moment he sat, listening. "Riders," he said tersely, "coming from behind us." Quickly he pulled the horses off the road and had barely made the heavy brush when a large group of blue-clad riders swept past them. Jamie sat erect in the saddle and watched with burning eyes. The drawn, tight lines of his face showed that only the pain had kept him conscious.

"Josey, them fellers ride like the Second Colorado."

"Well," Josey drawled, "yore eyes is fine. Them boys is right pert fighters, but they couldn't track a litter of pigs 'crost a kitchen floor." He searched the boy's face as he spoke and was rewarded with a tight grin. "But," he added, "jest in case they can, we're leavin' the road. That line of woods means the Blackwater, and we're goin' to take a rest."

As he spoke, Josey turned the horses toward the river. With a casual joke he had hidden from the boy their alarming position. One look at Jamie in the light showed his weakness. He had to have rest, if nothing more. The horses were too tired to run if they were jumped, and the appearance of soldiers from the north meant the alarm was to be spread south. They figured him for heading to the Nations. This time they figured him right.

4

The heavy timbered approaches to the Blackwater afforded a welcome refuge from the open rolling prairie over which they had come. Josey found a shallow stream that ran toward the river and guided the horses down it, knee-deep in water. Fifty yards back from the sluggish Blackwater he brought the horses up the bank of the stream and pushed through heavy sumac vines until he found a small glade sunken between banks lined with elm and gum trees. He helped Jamie from the saddle, but the boy's legs buckled under him. Josey carried him in his arms to a place where the bank overhung the glade. There he lay blankets and stretched Jamie out on his back. He pulled the saddles from the horses and picketed them with lariats on the lush grass of the marshy ravine. When he returned, Jamie was sleeping, his face flushed with the beginning of fever.

It was high noon when Jamie wakened. The pain washed over him in heavy throbs that tore at his chest. He saw Josey hunched over a tiny fire, feeding the fire with one hand as he maneuvered a heavy tin cup over the flame with the other. Seeing Jamie awake, he came to him with the cup, and cradling the boy's head in his arms, he pressed the cup to his lips. "A little Tennessee rifle-ball tonic, Jamie," he said.

Jamie swallowed and coughed, "Tastes like you made it with rifle balls," and he managed a weak grin.

Josey tilted more of the hot liquid down his throat. "Sass'fras and iron root, with a dab of side meat . . . we ain't got no beef," he said and eased the boy's head back on the blanket. "Yonder, in Tennessee, every time there was a shootin' scrape, Gran'ma commenced to boil up tonic. She'd send me to the hollers to dig sass'-fras and iron root. Reckin I dug enough roots to loosen all the ground in Carter County. Re'clect that oncet Pa been coughin' fit to kill fer a month of Sundays. Everybody said as how he had lung fever. Gran'ma commenced to feedin' him tonic ever' mornin'. Then one night Pa had a fit of coughin' and spit up a rifle ball on the pillarcase . . . next mornin' he felt goodern' a boar hawg chasin' a sow. Gran'ma said was the tonic done it."

Jamie's eyes closed, and he breathed with heavy, broken rhythm. Josey eased the tangled blond head down on the blanket. For the first time he noticed the long, almost girlish eyelashes, the smooth face.

"Grit an' sand, by God," he muttered. There was tenderness in the gesture as he smoothed the tousled hair with a rough hand. Josey sat back on his heels and looked thoughtfully into the cup. He frowned. The liquid was pink . . . blood, lung blood.

Josey watched the horses cropping grass without seeing them. He was thinking of Jamie. Too many times, in a hundred fights, he had seen men choke on their blood from pierced lungs. The nearest help was the Nations. He had been through the Cherokee's land several times on the trail to Texas and back. Once he had met General Stand Watie, the Cherokee General of the Confederacy. He knew many of the warriors well and once had joined with them as outriders to General Jo Shelby's Cavalry when Shelby raided north along the Kansas Border. The bone-handled knife that protruded from the top of his left boot had been given him by the Cherokee. On its handle was inscribed the Wanton mark that only proven braves could wear. He trusted the Cherokee, and he trusted his medicine.

Although he had heard that the Federals were moving in on the Cherokee's land because of their siding with the Confederates, he knew the Indian would not be easily moved and that he still controlled most of the territory. Jamie had to be gotten to the Cherokee. There was no other help. In his mind Josey sketched the map of the country he knew so well. There were sixty miles of broken, rolling prairie between him and the Grand River. Beyond the Grand was the haven of the Ozarks that could be skirted but was always near at hand for safety . . . all the way to the border of the Nations.

Gathering clouds had moved over the sun. Where it had been warm, a brisk wind picked up from the north and brought a chill. Josey was reluctant to wake the boy, who was still sleeping. He decided to wait another hour, bringing them closer to the dusk of eve-

ning. It was pleasant in the glade. The light wash of
the river was constant in the distance. A redheaded
woodpecker set to hammering on an elm, and brush
wrens chattered, gathering grass seeds in the ravine.

Josey rose and stretched his arms. He knelt to pull
the blanket higher around Jamie, and in that split instant the chill warning of silence ran cold over him.
The brush wrens flew up in a brown cloud. The woodpecker disappeared around the tree. He moved his
hand toward the holstered right pistol as he turned his
head upward to the opposite bank and looked into the
barrels of rifles held by two bearded men.

"Now you jest do that, cousin," the taller one spoke.
He had the rifle to shoulder and was sighting down
the barrel. "You bring that ol' pistol right out."

Josey looked at them steadily but didn't move. They
weren't soldiers. Both wore dirty overalls and non-
descript jackets. The tall one had mean eyes that
burned down the rifle barrel at Josey. The shorter of
the two held his rifle more loosely.

"This here is him, Abe," the short one spoke. "That's
Josey Wales. I seen him at Lone Jack with Bloody Bill.
He's meaner'n a rattler and twicet as fast with them
pistols."

"Yore a real tush hawg, ain't ye, Wales?" Abe said
sarcastically. "What's the matter with that'n laying
down?"

Josey didn't answer but gazed steadily back at the
two. He watched the wind flutter a red bandanna
around the throat of Abe.

"Tell you what, Mr. Wales," Abe said, "you put yore
hands top of yore head and stand up facin' me."

Josey clasped his hands on top of his hat, stood
slowly, and squared about to face the men. His right
knee trembled slightly.

"Watch him, Abe," the short man half yelled, "I seen him. . . ."

"Shut up, Lige," Abe said roughly. "Now, Mr. Wales, I'd as soon shoot ye now, 'ceptin' it'll be harder to drag ye through the brush to where's we can git our pound price fer ye. Move yore left hand down and unbuckle that pistol belt. Make it slow 'nough I kin count the hairs on yer hand."

As Josey slowly lowered his hand to the belt buckle, his left shoulder moved imperceptibly beneath the buckskin jacket. The movement tilted forward the .36 Navy Colt beneath his arm. The gun belt fell. From the corner of his eye Josey saw Jamie, still sleeping beneath the blanket.

Abe sighed in relief. "There, ye see, Lige, when ye pull his teeth he's tame as a heel hound. I always wanted to face out one of these big pistol fighters they raise all the fuss about. It's all in the way ye handle 'em. Now ye call up Benny back there on the horse."

Lige half turned, his eyes still darting back at Josey. With his free hand he cupped his mouth, "Bennnnny! Come up . . . we got 'em." In the distance a horse crashed through the undergrowth, moving toward them.

Josey felt the looseness come over him that marks the fighter, natural born. He coolly measured the distance while his brain toted up the chances for a pistolman. He was past the first tense moment. His adversaries had relaxed; there was a third coming up. This caused a slight distraction, but he needed another before the third man arrived. For the first time he spoke . . . so suddenly that Abe jumped. "Listen, Mister," he said in a half-whining, placating tone, "there's gold in them saddlebags . . ." he brought his right hand easily from his head to point at the saddles, "and you can . . ."

In midsentence he rolled his body with the quickness of a cat. His right hand was already snaking out the Navy as his body flipped over down the bank. The rifle shot dug the ground where he had been. It was the only shot Abe made. The Navy was spitting flame from a rolling, dodging target. Once, twice, three times . . . faster than a man could count, Josey fanned the hammer. The glade was filled with a solid roar of sound. Abe pitched forward, down the bank. Lige staggered backward into a tree and sat down. Blood spurted like a fountain from his chest. He never got off a shot.

Out of the roll, Josey came to his feet, running up the bank and into the undergrowth; but the frightened horseman had wheeled his mount and fled. Returning, Josey rolled the facedown Abe over on his back. He noted with satisfaction the two neat holes made by the Navy, less than an inch apart in the center of Abe's chest. Lige sat against the tree, his face frozen in startled surprise. His left eye stared blankly at the treetops, and where his right eye had been, there was a round, bloody cavern.

"Caught 'em a mite high," Josey grunted and then noticed the gaping hole in Lige's chest. He turned. Halfway down the opposite bank, Jamie lay prone on his stomach, a .44 Colt in his right hand. He grinned weakly back at Josey.

"I knowed ye'd go fer the big 'un first, Josey. I shaded ye by a hair on that 'un."

Josey came across the glade and looked down at the boy. "If ye've started them holes in ye to leakin' agin, I'm goin' to whup ye with a knotted plow line."

"They ain't, Josey, honest. I feel pert as a ruttin'

buck." Jamie tried to rise, and his knees buckled under him. He sat down. Josey walked to the saddlebags and brought back a small bag. He handed the bag to Jamie.

"Jaw on this side meat and 'pone while 1 saddle the horses," he commanded. "We got to ride, boy. Thet feller rode out'n here won't let his shirttail hit his back 'til he's got mobs after us all over hell and Sunday." Josey was moving as he talked, cinching saddles, checking the horses, retrieving his holstered pistols, and finally reloading the .36 Navy.

"We got near fifty mile to the South Grand. Most of it is open with no more'n a gully ever' ten mile to hide a hoss. Them Colorado boys rode south . . . spreadin' word and roustin' out all the jaspers after reeward money. Now," he said grimly, "they'll know fer sure, we're headed south."

A fit of coughing seized Jamie as Josey lifted him into the saddle, and Josey watched with alarm as blood tinted his lips. He swung on his horse beside the boy.

"Ye know, Jamie," he said, "I know a feller lives in a cabin at the fork of the Grand and Osage. Ye'd be safe there and ye could lay out awhile. I could show m'self back upcountry and . . ."

"I reckin not," Jamie interrupted. His voice was weak, but there was no mistaking the dogged stubbornness.

"Ye damn little fool," Josey exploded, "I ain't totin' ye all over hell's creation and ye dribblin' blood over half Missouri. I got better things to do. . . ." Josey's voice trailed off. Anxiety in his tone had crept past his seeming outrage.

Jamie knew. "I tote my end of the log," he said weakly, "an' I'm stickin', slap to Texas."

Josey snatched the reins of the mare and started the horses toward the river. As they passed the sprawled figure of Abe, Jamie said, "Wisht we had time to bury them fellers."

"To hell with them fellers," Josey snarled. He spat a stream of tobacco juice into Abe's upturned face, "Buzzards got to eat, same as worms."

5

They followed the river bank downstream, away from Warrensburg, and crossed at a shallows belly-deep to the horses. Coming out of the river, they pushed at a walk through a half mile of thick bottom growth before they came up to thinning timber. It was two hours until sundown, and before them lay the open prairie broken only by rolling mounds. To their right was Warrensburg with the Clinton road running south; a road they couldn't use now.

Josey pulled the horses up in the last shelter of trees. He scanned the sky. Rain would help. It always helped to drive undisciplined mobs and posses back indoors. Although the clouds were thickening, there was no immediate promise of rain. The wind was brisking stronger out of the north, cold and sharp, bending the waist-high bushes across the prairie.

Still they sat their horses. Josey watched a dust cloud in the distance and followed it until it petered out . . . it was the wind. He studied the rolls of mounds and came back to study them again . . . giving time for any horsemen to come into view who might have been hidden. All the way to the horizon . . . there were no riders. Josey untied a blanket from behind his saddle and brought it around the hunched shoulders of Jamie. He tugged the cavalry hat lower to his eyes.

"Let's ride," he said tersely and moved the roan out. The little mare fell in behind. The horses were rested and strong. Josey had to hold the roan down to a walk to prevent the shorter-legged mare from breaking into a trot.

Jamie urged the mare up alongside Josey. "Don't hold back 'count of me, Josey," he yelled weakly against the wind, "I kin ride."

Josey pulled the horses up. "I ain't holdin' back 'count of you, ye thickheaded grasshopper," he said evenly. "Fust place, if we run these hosses, we'll kick up dust, second place they's enough posses in south Missouri after us to start another war, and in the third place, ye try runnin' 'stead of thinkin' and they'll swing us on a rope by dark. We got to wolf our way through."

A half hour of steady pace brought them to a deep wash that split their path and ran westward. Choked with thick brush and stunted cedar, it afforded good cover, but Josey guided the horses directly across and up onto the prairie again. "They'll curry-comb them washes . . . anyways, that'n ain't goin' in our direction," he remarked dryly.

A hundred yards farther and he stopped the horses.

Stepping down, he retrieved a brush top from the ground and retraced their steps back to the wash. Carefully as a housewife, he backed, sweeping away the hoofprints in the loose soil. "Iff'n they pick up our trail, and they're dumb enough . . . they could lose two hours in thet wash," he told Jamie as he swung the horses forward again.

Another hour, steadily southward. Jamie no longer lifted his head to scan the horizon. Jolting, searing pain filled his body. He could feel the swelling of his flesh over the tightly wrapped bandage. The clouds were lowering, heavier and darker, and the wind carried a distinct taste of moistness. Dusk of evening lent an eerie light to the wind-whipped prairie brush that made the landscape look alive.

Suddenly Josey halted the horses. "Riders," he said tersely, "comin' from behind us." Jamie listened, but he heard nothing . . . then, a faint drumming of hooves. Far ahead, perhaps five or six miles, there was a knoll of thick woods. Too far. There was no other cover offered.

Josey stepped down. "A dozen, maybe more, but they ain't fanned out . . . they're bunched and headin' fer them woods yonder."

Carefully, with unhurried calm, he lifted Jamie from the saddle and sat him spraddle-legged on the ground. Leading the roan close to the boy, he seized the horse's nose with his left hand, and throwing his right arm over its head, he grabbed the roan's ear. He twisted viciously. The roan's knees trembled and buckled . . . and he rolled to the ground. Josey extended a hand to Jamie and pulled the boy to the horse's head. "Lay 'crost his neck, Jamie, and hold his nose."

Leaping to his feet, Josey grabbed the head of the mare. But she fought him, backing and kicking, swinging him off the ground. Her eyes rolling, and frothing at the mouth, she almost bolted loose from his grip. Once, he reached for the boot knife but had to quickly renew his hold to prevent the horse from breaking away. The hoofbeats of the posse were now distinct and growing in sound. Desperately, Josey swung his feet off the ground. Still holding the mare's head, he locked his legs around her neck and pulled his body downward on her head. Her nose dragged into the dirt. She tried to plunge, lost her footing, and fell heavily on her side.

Josey lay as he had fallen, his legs wrapped around the mare's neck, holding her head tightly against his chest. He had fallen not three feet from Jamie. Facing the boy, he could see the white face and feverish eyes as he lay chest-down over the roan's neck. The drumming beat of the posse's horses now made the ground vibrate.

"Can ye hear me, boy?" Josey's whisper was hoarse.

Jamie's white face nodded.

"Listen, now . . . listen. Iff'n ye see me jump up, ye stay down. I'll take the mare . . . but ye stay down 'til ye hear shootin' and runnin' back toward the river. Then ye lay back on thet roan. He'll git up with ye. Ye ride south. Ye hear me, boy?"

The feverish eyes stared back at him. The thin face set in stubborn lines. Josey cursed softly under his breath.

The riders came on. The horses were being cantered, their hooves beating rhythmically on the ground. Now Josey could hear the creak of saddle leather, and from his prone position he saw the body of horsemen loom into view. They passed not a dozen yards from the flattened horses. Josey could see their hats . . . their shoulders, silhouetted against the lighter horizon.

Jamie coughed. Josey looked at the boy and slipped the thong from a Colt and held the pistol in his hand across the head of the mare. Blood trickled from the mouth of Jamie, and Josey saw him heave to cough again. Then he watched as the boy lowered his head; he was biting into the roan's neck. Still the riders came by in a maddening eternity. Blood was dripping now from the nose of Jamie as his body heaved for air.

"Turn loose, Jamie," Josey whispered, "turn loose, damn ye, or ye'll die." Still the boy held on. The last of the riders moved from view, and the hoofbeats of their horses faded. Josey stretched to his full length and hit Jamie a brutal blow against his head. The boy rolled on his side and his chest expanded with air. He was unconscious.

Rising to his feet, Josey brought the mare up where she stood, head down and trembling. He pulled Jamie from the roan, and the big horse rose, snorted, and shook himself. He bent over the boy and wiped the blood from his face and neck. Lifting his shirt, he saw a mass of horribly discolored flesh bulging over the tight wrappings. He loosened the bandages and from his canteen he patted cold water over Jamie's face.

The boy opened his eyes. He grinned tightly up at Josey and from behind set teeth he whispered, "Whupped 'em agin, didn't we, Josey?"

"Yeah," Josey said softly, "we whupped 'em agin."

He rolled a blanket and placed it under Jamie's head and stood facing southward. The posse had disappeared into the closing darkness. Still he watched. After a long time he was rewarded with the flickering of campfires from the woods to the southwest. The posse was encamping for the night.

Had he been alone, Josey would have drifted back toward the Blackwater and with the morning followed the posse south. But Josey had seen mortification in wounded men before. It always killed. He figured a hundred miles to the Cherokee's medicine lodge.

Jamie was sitting up, and Josey lifted him onto the mare. They continued southward, passing the lights of the posse's camp on their right.

Though the sky was dark with clouds Josey calculated midnight when he brought the horses to a halt. Though conscious, Jamie swayed in the saddle, and Josey lashed his feet in the stirrups, bringing the rope under the horse's belly to secure the boy.

"Jamie," he said, "the mare's got a smooth single-foot gait. Nearly smooth as a walk. We got to make more time. Can ye handle it, boy?"

"I can handle it." The voice came weak but confident. Josey lifted the roan into a slow, mile-eating canter, and the little mare stayed with him. The undulating prairie slowly changed character . . . a small, tree-bunched hillock showed here and there. Before dawn they had reached the Grand River. Searching its banks for a ford, Josey picked a well-traveled trail to cross and then pushed on across open ground toward the Osage.

They nooned on the banks of the Osage River. Josey grained the horses from the corn in Jamie's saddlebags. Now, to the south and east, they could see the foothills of the wild Ozark Mountains with the tangled ravines and uncountable ridges that long had served the outlaw on the run. They were close, but the Osage was too deep and too wide.

Over a tiny flame Josey steamed broth for Jamie. For himself, he wolfed down half-cooked salt pork and corn pone. Jamie rested on the ground; the broth had brought color to his cheeks.

"How we goin' to cross, Josey?"

"There's a ferry 'bout five mile down, at Osceola crossing," Josey answered as he cinched the saddles on the horses.

"How in thunderation we goin' to git acrost on a ferry?" Jamie asked incredulously.

Josey lifted the boy into the saddle. "Well," he drawled, "ye jest git on it and ride, I reckin."

Heavy timber laced with persimmon and stunted cedar bushes shielded them from the clearing. The ferry was secured to pilings on the bank. Back from the river there were two log structures, one of which appeared to be a store. Josey could see the Clinton road snaking north for a half mile until it disappeared over a rolling rise and reappeared in the distance.

Light wood smoke drifted from the chimneys of both the store and the dwelling, but there were no signs of life except an old man seated on a stump near the ferry. Josey watched him for a long time. The old man was weaving a wire fish basket. He looked up constantly from his work to peer back toward the Clinton road.

"Old man acts nervous," Josey muttered, "and this here would be a likely place."

Jamie slumped beside him on the mare. "Likely fer . . . reckin things ain't right?"

"I'd give a yaller-wheeled red waggin to see on the other side of them cabins," Josey said . . . then, "Come on." With the practiced audacity of the guerrilla, he walked his horse from the brush straight toward the old man.

6

For nearly ten years old man Carstairs had run the ferry. He owned it . . . the store and the house, bought with his own scrimped-up savings, by God. For all of that time old man Carstairs had walked a tightrope. Ferrying Kansas Redleg, Missouri guerrilla, Union Cavalry . . . once he had even ferried a contingent of Jo Shelby's famous Confederate riders. He could whistle "Battle Hymn of the Republic" or "Dixie" with equal enthusiasm, depending upon present company. Morning and night these many years, he had berated the old lady, "Them regular army ones ain't so bad. But them Redlegs and guerrillas is mad dogs . . . ye hear! Mad dogs! Ye look sidewise at 'em . . . they'll kill us all . . . burn us out."

With cunning he had survived. Once he had seen

Quantrill, Joe Hardin, and Frank James. They and seventy-five guerrillas were dressed in Yankee uniforms. They had questioned him as to his sympathies, but the old man's crafty eyes had spotted a "guerrilla shirt" under the open blue blouse of one of the men . . . and he had cursed the Union. He had never seen Bloody Bill or Jesse James . . . or Josey Wales, and the men that rode with them, but their reputations transcended Quantrill's in Missouri.

Only this morning he had ferried across two separate posses of horsemen who were searching for Wales and another outlaw. They had said he was in this area and all south Missouri was up in arms. Three thousand dollars! A lot of money . . . but they could have it . . . fer the likes of a gunslingin' killer sich as Wales. That is . . . unless . . .

Cavalry would be coming down the road any minute now. Carstairs looked around. It was then he saw the horsemen approaching. They had come out of the brush along the river bank, an alarming fact in itself. But the appearance of the lead horseman was even more alarming to Carstairs. He was astride a huge roan stallion that looked half wild. He approached to within ten feet and stopped. High top boots, fringed buckskin, the man was lean and had an air of wolfish hunger about him. He wore two holstered .44's, and the guns were tied down. Several days' growth of black beard stubbled his face below the mustache, and a gray cavalry hat was pulled low over the hardest black eyes old man Carstairs had ever seen. The old man shuddered as from a chill and sat frozen, the fish basket suspended outward in his hands . . . as though he were offering it as a gift.

"Howdy," the horseman said easily.

"Well, how . . . howdy," Carstairs fumbled. He felt numb. He watched, fascinated, as the horseman slid a long knife from his boot top, cut a wad of tobacco from a twist, and fed it into his mouth.

"Figgered we might give ye a mite of ferryin' business," the horseman said slowly past the chew.

"Why shore, shore." Old man Carstairs stood up.

"But . . . " the horseman caught him short, in the act of rising, "so's there won't be nothin' mistooken, I'm Josey Wales . . . and this here's my partner. We're jest a hair pushed fer time and we need a tad of things first."

"Why, Mr. Wales." Carstairs rose. His lips trembled uncontrollably, so that the forced smile appeared alternately as a sneer and a laugh. Inwardly he cursed his trembling. Dropping the fish basket, he managed to step toward the horse, extending his hand. "My name's Carstairs, Sim Carstairs. I've heard tell of ye, Mr. Wales. Bill Quantrill was a good friend of mine . . . mighty good friend, we'uns. . . ."

"T'ain't a sociable visit, Mr. Carstairs," Josey said flatly, "who all ye got hereabouts?"

"Why nobody," Carstairs was eager, "thet is 'cept the old lady there in the house and Lemuel, my hired hand. He ain't right bright, Mr. Wales . . . runs his mouth and sich . . . he's there, in the store."

"Tell ye what," Josey said as he pitched five bright double eagles at the feet of Carstairs, "me and you will amble on up to the house and the store. I got a tech of cramp . . . so I'll ride. When we git there, ye don't go inside . . . but ye step to the door and tell the missus that we got to have CLEAN bandages . . . lots of 'em. We got to have a boiled-up poultice fer a bullet wound . . . and hurry."

The old man looked askance at Josey, and receiving a nod he quickly gathered the gold coins out of the dust and moved at a half trot toward the house.

Josey turned to Jamie behind him, "You stay here and keep the corners of them buildings under eyes." He put the roan on the heels of the old man. Stopping the horse at the porch of the log cabin, he listened while Carstairs shouted instructions through the open door of the cabin. Then as the old man turned from the door, "Let's step over to the store, Mr. Carstairs. Tell yore feller in there we want a half side of bacon, ten pound of beef jerky, and twenty pound of horse grain."

Carstairs returned with the bags, and Josey had just settled the grain behind his saddle when a tiny white-haired woman stepped through the door of the cabin. She held a pipe in her mouth and extended a clean pillowcase stuffed with the bandages toward Josey.

Moving his horse to the edge of the porch, Josey tipped his hat. "Howdy, ma'am," he said quietly, and reaching for the pillowcase he placed two twenty-dollar gold coins in her small hand. "I thank ye kindly, ma'am," he said.

Sharp blue eyes quickened in the wrinkled face. She took the pipe from her mouth. "Ye'll be Josey Wales, I reckin."

"Yes, ma'am, I'm Josey Wales."

"Well," the old lady held him with her eyes, "them poultices be laced with feather moss and mustard root. Mind ye, drap water on 'em occasional to keep 'em damp." Then without pause she continued, "Reckin ye know they're a-goin' to heel and hide ye to a barn door."

A faint smile lifted the scar on Josey's face. "I've heard tell of sich talk, ma'am."

He touched his hat . . . whirled the roan and followed the old man to the ferry. As they walked their horses aboard the flat, he looked back. She was still standing . . . and he thought she gave a secret wave of her hand . . . but she could have pushed a strand of hair back from her face.

Old man Carstairs felt bold enough to grumble as he walked the couple cable from bow to stern on the ferry. "Usually have Lem here to help. This here is heavy work fer one old man."

But he moved the ferry on out across the river. To the north a distinct rumble of thunder rolled across the darkening clouds. As the current caught the ferry they moved more swiftly on a downward angle; and half an hour later, Josey was leading the horses onto the opposite bank and into the trees.

It was Jamie who saw them first. His shout startled Carstairs, who was resting against a piling, and made Josey whirl in his tracks. Jamie was pointing back across the river. There, from the bank they had just left, was a large body of Union Cavalry, blue uniforms standing out against the horizon. They were waving their arms frantically.

Josey grinned, "Well, I'll be a suck-aig hound."

Jamie laughed . . . coughed and laughed again, "Whupped 'em agin, Josey," he said jubilantly . . . "We whupped 'em agin."

Carstairs didn't share in the enthusiasm. He scrambled up the bank to Josey. "They're hollerin' fer me to come over . . . I got to go . . . I cain't hold up." A gleam touched his eyes . . . "but I'll hold up 'til ya'll are out of sight . . . even longer. I'll make do somethin's wrong. You fellers git goin', quick."

Josey nodded and headed the horses up through the

trees. Only a short distance, and undergrowth blocked their view of the river. Here he halted the horses.

"Thet feller ain't goin' to hold up thet ferry . . . he's goin' to bring that cavalry over," Jamie said.

Josey looked up at the lowering clouds. "I know," he said, "wants hisself a piece of the reeward." He brought the horses about . . . back to the river.

Carstairs had already moved the ferry from the bank. Walking the cable at a half trot, he was making rapid time toward midstream. Across the river a blue-clad knot of men were pulling on the ferry's cable.

Josey dismounted. From a saddlebag he pulled nose bags for the horses, poured grain into them, and fastened them over the mouths of the horses. The big roan stomped his hooves in satisfaction. Jamie watched the ferry as it neared the opposite bank . . . the shouts of the men came faintly to their ears as fully half of the cavalry present boarded the ferry.

"They're comin'," Jamie said.

Josey was busying himself checking the hooves of the munching horses, lifting first one and then another foot. "From the tracks, t'other side, I'd cal'clate forty, fifty hosses was brought acrost this mornin'," he said, "and they're ahead of us. Reckin we need to space a little time 'twixt them and us."

Jamie watched the ferry moving toward them. Soldiers were walking the cable. " 'Pears to me we're goin' to be needin' a little space behint us too," he said bleakly.

Josey straightened to look. The ferry was almost to midstream, and as they watched, the current began to catch, pulling the cable in a taut curve. Josey slid the .56 Sharps from the saddle boot.

"Hold Big Red," he said as he handed the horse's

reins to Jamie. For a long time he sighted down the barrel . . . then . . . BOOM! The heavy rifle reverberated in echo across the river. All activity stopped on the ferry. The men stood motionless, frozen in motion. The cable parted from the pilings with a snap of telegraphic *zing* of sound. For a moment the ferry in the middle of the river floated motionless, suspended. Slowly it began to swing downstream. Faster and faster, as the current picked up its load of men and horses. Now there was shouting . . . men dashed first to one end and then the other in confusion. Two horses jumped over the side and swam about in a circle.

"Godalmighty!" Jamie breathed.

The confused tangle of shouting men and pitching horses was carried at locomotive speed . . . farther and farther . . . until they disappeared around the trees of the river bend.

"That there," Josey grinned, "is called a Missouri boat ride."

Still they waited, letting the horses finish the grain. Across river they saw a mad dash of blue cavalrymen head south down the river bank.

From the Osage Josey turned the horses southwest along the banks of the Sac River. Across the Sac was more open prairie, but on their left was the comforting wilderness of the Ozarks. Once, in late afternoon, they sighted a large body of horsemen heading southwest, across the river, and they held their horses until the drumming hoofbeats had died in the distance. North of Stockton they forded the Sac, and nightfall caught them on the banks of Horse Creek, north of Jericho Springs.

Josey guided the horses up a shallow spring that fed the creek, into a tangled ravine. One mile, two, he traveled, halting only when the ravine narrowed to a thin slash in the side of the mountain. High above them trees whipped in a fierce wind, but here there was a calmness broken only by the gurgling of water over rocks.

The narrow gorge was choked with brush and scuppernong vines. Elm, oak, hickory, and cedar grew profusely. It was in a sheltered clump of thick cedar that he threw blankets and Jamie, lying in the warm quietness, fell asleep. Josey unsaddled the horses, grained and picketed them near the spring. Then close to Jamie he dug an "outlaw's oven," a foot-deep hole in the ground with flat stones edged over the top. Three feet from the fire no light was visible, but the heated stones and flames beneath quickly cooked the pan of side meat and boiled the jerky broth.

As he worked he attuned his ears to the new sounds of the ravine. Without looking, he knew there was a nest of cardinals in the persimmon bushes across the branch; a flicker grutted from the trunk of an elm and the brush wrens whispered in the undergrowth. Farther back, up the hollow, a screech owl had taken up its precisely timed woman's wail of anguish. These were the rhythms he placed in his subconscious. The high wind whining above him . . . the feathery whisper of breeze through the cedars . . . this was the melody. But if the rhythm broke . . . the birds were his sentinels.

He had eaten and fed Jamie the broth. Now he heated water and wet the poultices. When he took the old bandages from around Jamie, the big hole in his chest was blotched with blue flesh turning black. "Proud" flesh speckled the wound in puffy whiteness. The boy kept his eyes from the mangled chest, looking steadily up to Josey's face.

"It ain't bad, is it, Josey?" he asked quietly.

Josey was cleaning the wound with hot rags. "It's bad," he said evenly.

"Josey?"

"Yeah."

"Back there, on the Grand . . . thet was the fastest shootin' I ever seed. I never shaded ye. Na'ar bit."

Josey didn't answer as he placed the poultices and wrapped the bandages around the boy.

"Iff'n I don't make it, Josey," Jamie hesitated, "I want ye to know I'm prouder'n a game rooster to have rid with ye."

"Ye are a game rooster, son," Josey said roughly, "now shet up."

Jamie grinned. He closed his eyes, and the shadows quickly softened the hollowed cheeks. In sleep he was a little boy.

Josey felt the heavy drag of exhaustion. In three days he had slept only in brief dozes in the saddle. His eyes had begun to play tricks on him, seeing the "gray wolves" that weren't there . . . and hearing the sounds that couldn't be. Time to hole up. He knew the feeling well. As he rolled into his blankets, back in the brush, away from Jamie and the horses, he thought of the boy . . . and his mind wandered back to his own boyhood in the Tennessee mountains.

There was Pa, lean and mountain-learned, settin' on a stump. "Them as won't fight fer their own kind, ain't worth their sweat salt," he had said.

"I reckin," the little boy Josey had nodded.

And there was Pa, layin' a hand on his shoulder when he was a stripling . . . and Pa wa'ant give to show feelin's. He had stood up to the McCabes down at the settlement . . . and them with the sheriff on their side. Pa had looked at him, close and proud.

"Gittin' on to be a man," Pa had said. "Always re'clect to be proud of yer friends . . . but fight fer sich as ye kin be prouder of yer enemies." Proud, by God.

Well, Josey thought drowsily . . . the enemies was damn shore the right kind, and the friend . . . the boy . . . all sand grit and cucklebur. He slept.

A brief splatter of rain wakened him. There was the ghostly light of predawn made dimmer by dark clouds that rushed ahead of the wind. Light fog trapped in the ravine added to the ghostly air. It was colder. Josey could feel the chill through his blanket. Overhead the wind whined and beat the treetops. Josey rolled from his blanket. The horses were watering at the spring. He grained them and coaxed a flame alive in the fire hole. Kneeling beside Jamie with hot jerky broth, he shook the boy awake. But when his eyes opened, there was no recognition in them.

"I told Pa," the boy said weakly, "that yaller heifer would make the best milker in Arkansas. Four gallon if she gives a drap." He paused, listening intently . . . then, a chuckle of laughter. "Reckin that red bon's a cheater, Pa . . . done left the pack and jumped that ol' fox's trail."

Suddenly he sat up wildly, his eyes frightened. Josey placed a restraining hand on his shoulder. "Pa said it was Jennison, Ma. Jennison! A hunnert men!" Just as suddenly he collapsed back onto the blankets. Sobs racked him, and great tears ran down his cheeks. "Ma," he said brokenly, "Ma." And he was still . . . his eyes closed.

Josey looked down at the boy. He knew Jamie had come from Arkansas, but he had never discussed his reasons for joining the guerrillas. Nobody did. Doc Jennison! Josey knew he had carried his Redleg raids into Arkansas where he had looted and burned so

many farmhouses that the lonely chimneys left standing became known as "Jennison Monuments." The
hatred rose again inside him.

As he raised Jamie's head to feed him the broth the
nightmare had passed, but he could feel that the boy
was weaker as he lifted him into the saddle. Once
more he lashed Jamie's feet to the stirrups. He figured
sixty miles to the border of the Nations, and he knew
that troops and posses were gathering in growing
numbers to block his reckless ride.

"Reckin they figger me fer plumb loco," Josey muttered as he rode, "fer not takin' to the hills." But the
hills meant sure death for Jamie. There was a narrow
chance with the Cherokee.

His simple code of loyalty disallowed any thought of
his own safety at the sacrifice of a friend. He could
have turned into the mountains on the off chance that
help could be found for the boy . . . and he himself
would have been safe in the wildness. For men of a
lesser code it would have been sufficient. The question
never entered the outlaw's mind. For all their craft
and guerrilla cunning, tacticians would consider this
code as such men's greatest weakness . . . but on the
other side of the coin the code accounted for their
fierceness as warriors, their willingness to "charge hell
with a bucket of water," as they were once described
in Union Army reports.

The tactical weakness in Josey's case was apparent.
The Union Army and posses knew his partner was
desperately wounded. They knew he could get medi-
cal help only in the Nations. His mastery of the pistols,
his cunning born of a hundred running fights, his guerrilla boldness and audacity, had carried him and Jamie
through a roused countryside, but they also knew the
code of these hardened pistol fighters. Where they

could not divine the mind and tricks of the wolf, they knew his instinct. And so horsemen were pounding toward the border of the Nations to converge and meet him. They knew Josey Wales.

7

The cold dawn found them riding across an open space of prairie ground, the mountains to their left. Before noon they forded Horse Creek and continued southwest, staying close to the timbered ridges, but Josey keeping the horses on dangerous open ground. Time was the enemy of Jamie Burns. Shortly after noon Josey rested the horses in thick timber. Placing strips of jerky beef in Jamie's mouth, he gruffly instructed, "Chaw on it, but don't swaller nothin' but juice."

The boy nodded but didn't speak. His face was beginning to take on a puffiness, and swelling enlarged his neck. Once, far to their right, they saw dust rising of many horses, but the riders never came into view.

By late afternoon they had forded Dry Fork and

were crossing, at an easy canter, a long roll of prairie. Josey pulled to a halt and pointed behind them. It appeared to be a full squad of cavalry. Although they were several miles away, the soldiers had apparently spotted the fugitives, for as Josey and Jamie watched, they spurred their horses into a gallop. Josey could easily have sought shelter in the wild mountains not a half mile on their left, but that would mean hard . . . slow traveling, rather than the five miles of prairie they had before them. In the distance a tall spur of mountain extended before them over the prairie.

"We'll make fer that mountain straight ahead," Josey said. He brought his horse close to Jamie. "Now listen. Them fellers ain't shore yet who we are. I'm goin' to make 'em shore. When I shoot at 'em . . . you let that little mare canter . . . but ye hold 'er down. When ye hear me shoot agin . . . ye turn 'er loose. Ye understand?" Jamie nodded. "I want them soldier boys to run them horses into the ground," he added grimly as he slid the big Sharps from the saddle boot.

Without aiming, he fired. The echoes boomed back from the mountain. The effect was almost instantaneous on the loping cavalrymen. They lifted their arms, and their horses stretched out in a dead run. The mare set off in an easy canter that rapidly left Josey behind. The big roan sensed the excitement and wanted to run, but Josey held him down to a bone-jarring, high-step trot.

There was a distance of a half mile . . . now three-quarters . . . now a mile separating the cantering mare from him. Behind, he could hear the first faint beating of running horses. Still he jogged. The drumming of hooves became louder; now he could hear the faint shouts of the men. Slipping the knife from his boot, he carefully cut a plug of tobacco from the twist. As he cheeked the wad the hoofbeats grew louder.

"Well, Red," he drawled, "ye been snortin' to go . . ." he slid a Colt from a holster and fired into the air, ". . . now RUN!" The roan leaped. Ahead of him, Josey saw the mare gather haunches and settle lower as she flew over the ground. She was fast, but the roan was already gaining.

There was never any doubt. The big horse bounded like a cat over shallow washes, never breaking stride. Josey leaned low in the saddle, feeling the great power of the roan as he flew over the ground, closing the gap on the mare. He was less than a hundred yards behind her when she made the heavy timber of the ridge. As Josey pulled back on the roan, he turned and saw the cavalrymen . . . they were walking their horses, fully two miles behind him. Their mounts had been "bottomed out."

Jamie had pulled up in the timber, and as Josey reached him the heavy clouds opened up. A blinding, whipping rain obscured the prairie behind them. Lightning touched a timbered ridge, cracked with a blue-white light, and the deep rumbling that followed caught up the echoes and merged with more lightning stabs that made the roar continuous. Josey pulled slickers from behind their cantles.

"A real frog-strangler," and he wrapped a slicker around Jamie. The boy was conscious, but his face was twisted and white, and his body rigid in an effort to cling to the saddle.

Josey gripped his arm, "Fifteen, maybe twenty miles, Jamie, and we'll bed down in a warm lodge on the Neosho." He gently shook the boy. "We'll be in the Nations, another twenty miles . . . we'll have help."

Jamie nodded . . . but he did not speak. Josey pulled the reins of the mare from the clenched hands that held the saddle horn, and leading, moved the horses at a walk upward into the ridges.

The lightning flashes had stopped, but the rain still came, whipped into sheets by the wind. Darkness set in quickly, but Josey guided the roan with a sureness of familiarity with the mountains. The trails were dim now, that sought out the cuts between the ridges; that headed straight into a mountain only to turn and twist and find a hidden draw. They were still there . . . the trails he had followed with Anderson, going into and coming out of the Nations. The trails would carry him through the corner of Newton County and onto the river flats of the Neosho, out of Missouri.

The temperature fell. The rain lightened, and the breath of the horses made puffs of steam as they walked. It was after midnight before Josey called a halt to the steady pace. He saw the campfires below him . . . the half circle that hung like a necklace . . . enclosing the foothills of these mountains between him . . . and Jamie . . . and Neosho Basin a few miles away.

There was still some movement around the fires. As he squatted in the timber he could see an occasional figure outlined against the flame . . . and so he waited. Behind him the roan stamped an impatient foot, but the mare stood head down and tired. He dared not take Jamie from the saddle . . . there were only a few miles across the flats to the Nations . . . and a few more miles to the Neosho bottoms. There was a bitter-cold bite now in the wind, and the rain had almost stopped.

Patiently he watched, jaws slowly working at the tobacco. An hour passed, then another. Activity had died down around the campfires. There would be the pickets. Josey straightened and walked back to the horses. Jamie was slumped in the saddle, his chin resting on his chest. Josey clasped the boy's arm, "Jamie," but the moment his hand touched him, he knew. Jamie Burns was dead.

The realization of the boy's death came like a physical blow, so that his knees buckled and he actually staggered. He had known they would make it. The riding, the fighting against all odds . . . they HAD made it. They had whipped them all. Then for fate to snatch the boy from him. . . . Josey Wales cursed bitterly and long. He stretched his arms around the dead Jamie in the saddle . . . as if to warm him and bring him back . . . and he cursed at God until he choked on his own spittle.

His coughing brought back sanity, and he stood for a long time saying nothing. His bitterness subsided into thoughts of the boy who had stubbornly followed him with loyalty, who had died without a murmur. Josey removed his hat and stepping close to the mare placed his arm about the waist of Jamie. He looked up at the trees bending in the wind. "This here boy," he said gruffly, "was brung up in time of blood and dyin'. He never looked to question na'ar bit of it. Never turned his back on his folks 'ner his kind. He has rode with me, and I ain't got no complaints . . . " he paused, "Amen."

Moving with a sudden resolve, he untied the saddlebags from the mare and lashed them to his own saddle. He unbuckled the gunbelt from Jamie's waist and hung it over the roan's pommel. This done, he mounted the roan and led the mare, with the dead boy still in the saddle, down the ridge toward the campfires. At the bottom of the ridge he crossed a shallow creek and coming up from its bank found himself only fifty yards from the nearest campfire. There were pickets out, but they were dismounted, walking from fire to fire at a slow cadence.

Josey pulled the mare up beside the roan. He looped the reins back over the head of the horse and tied them tightly around the dead hands of Jamie that still gripped the saddle horn. Now he sidled the roan close, until his leg touched the leg of the boy.

"Bluebellies will give ye a better funeral, son," he said grimly, "anyways, we said we was goin' to the Nations . . . by God, one of us will git there."

Across the rump of the mare he laid a big Colt, so that when fired the powder burn would send her off. He took a deep breath, pulled his hat low, and fired the pistol.

The mare leaped from the burning pain and stampeded straight toward the nearest campfire. The reaction was almost instantaneous. Men ran toward the fires, rolling out of blankets, and hoarse, questioning shouts filled the air. Almost into the fire the mare ran, the grotesque figure on her back dipping and rolling with her motion . . . then she veered, still at a dead run, heading south along the creek bank. Men began to shoot, some kneeling with rifles, then rising to run on foot after the mare. Others mounted horses and dashed away down the creek.

Josey watched it all from the shadows. From far down the creek he heard more gunfire, followed by triumphant shouts. Only then did he walk the roan out of the trees, past the deserted campfires, and into the shadows that would carry him out of bloody Missouri.

And men would tell of this deed tonight around the campfires of the trail. They would save it for the last as they recounted the tales told of the outlaw Josey

Wales . . . using this deed to clinch the ruthlessness of the man. City men, who have no knowledge of such things, seeking only comfort and profit, would sneer in disgust to hide their fear. The cowboy, knowing the closeness of death, would gaze grimly into the camp-fire. The guerrilla would smile and nod his approval of audacity and stubbornness that carried a man through. And the Indian would understand.

PART 2

8

The cold air had brought heavy fog to the bottoms of the Neosho. Dawn was a pale light that ghosted through weird shapes of tree and brush, made unearthly in the gray thickness. There was no sun.

Lone Watie could hear the low rush of the river as it passed close by the rear of his cabin. The morning river sounds were routine and therefore good . . . the kingfisher and the bluejays that quarreled incessantly . . . the early caw of a crow-scout . . . once . . . that all was well. Lone Watie felt rather than thought of these things as he fried his breakfast of fish over a tiny flame in the big fireplace.

Like many of the Cherokees, he was tall, standing well over six feet in his boot moccasins that held, half tucked, the legs of buckskin breeches. At first glance he appeared emaciated, so spare was his frame . . . the doeskin shirt jacket flapping loosely about his body, the face bony and lacking in flesh, so that hollows of the cheeks added prominence to the bones and the hawk nose that separated intense black eyes capable of a cruel light. He squatted easily on haunches before the fire, turning the mealed fish in the pan with fluid movement, occasionally tossing back one of the black plaits of hair that hung to his shoulders.

The clear call of a nighthawk brought instant movement by the Indian. Nighthawks do not call in the light of day. He moved with silent litheness; taking his rifle, he glided to the rear door of the one-room cabin . . . dropped to belly and slid quickly into the brush. Again the call came, loud and clear.

As all mountain men know, the whippoorwill will not sing when the nighthawk is heard . . . and so now, from the brush, Lone answered with that whipping call.

Now there was silence. From his position in the brush Lone listened for the approach. Though only a few feet from the cabin he could scarcely see it. Sumac and dead honeysuckle vine had grown up the chimney and run over the roof. Brush and undergrowth had encroached almost to the walls. What once had been a trail had long since been covered over. One must know of this inaccessible hideout to whistle an approach.

The horse burst through the brush without warning. Lone was startled by the appearance of the big roan. He looked half wild with flaring nostrils and he stamped his feet as the rider reined him before the cabin door. He watched as the rider dismounted and casually turned his back to the cabin as he uncinched saddle and pulled it from the horse.

Lone's eyes ran over the man; the big, holstered

pistols, the boot knife, nor did he miss the slight bulge beneath the left shoulder. As the man turned he saw the white scar standing out of the black stubble and he noted the gray cavalry hat pulled low. Lone grunted with satisfaction; a fighting man who carried himself as a warrior should, with boldness and without fear.

The open buckskin jacket revealed something more that made Lone step confidently from the brush and approach him. It was the shirt; linsey-woolsey with a long open V that ended halfway down the waist with a rosette. It was the "guerrilla shirt," noted in U.S. Army dispatches as the only sure way to identify a Missouri guerrilla. Made by the wives, sweethearts, and womenfolk of the farms, it had become the uniform of the guerrilla. He always wore it . . . sometimes concealed . . . but always worn. Many of them bore fancy needlework and bright colors . . . this one was the plain color of butternut, trimmed in gray.

The man continued to rub down the roan, even as Lone walked toward him . . . and only turned when the Indian stopped silently, a yard away.

"Howdy," he said softly and extended his hand, "I'm Josey Wales."

"I have heard," Lone said simply, grasping the hand, "I am Lone Watie."

Josey looked sharply at the Indian. "I re'clect. I rode with ye oncet . . . and yer kinsman, General Stand Watie, 'crost the Osage and up into Kansas."

"I remember," Lone said, "it was a good fight" . . . and then . . . "I will stable your horse with mine down by the river. There is grain."

As he led the roan away Josey pulled his saddle and gear into the cabin. The floor was hard-packed dirt. The only furnishings were willows laid along the walls draped with blankets. Besides the cooking utensils there was nothing else, save the belt hanging by a peg that carried a Colt and long knife. The inevitable gray hat of the cavalry lay on a willow bed.

He remembered the cabin. After wintering at Mineral Creek, Texas, near Sherman, in '63, he had come back up the trail and had camped here. They had been told it was the farm of Lone Watie, but no one had been there . . . though there was evidence left of what had been a farm.

He knew something of the history of the Waties. They had lived in the mountains of north Georgia and Alabama. Stand Watie was a prominent Chief. Lone was a cousin. Dispossessed of their land by the U.S. government in the 1830's, they had walked with the Cherokee tribe on the "Trail of Tears" to the new land assigned them in the Nations. Nearly a third of the Cherokee had died on that long walk, and thousands of graves still marked the trail.

He had known the Cherokee as a small boy in the mountains of Tennessee. His father had befriended many of them who had hidden out, refusing to make the walk.

The mountain man did not have the "land hunger" of the flatlander who had instigated the government's action. He preferred the mountains to remain wild . . . free, unfettered by law and the irritating hypocrisy of organized society. His kinship, therefore, was closer to the Cherokee than to his racial brothers of the flatlands who strained mightily at placing the yoke of society upon their necks.

From the Cherokee he had learned how to hand-fish, easing his hands into the bank holes of the mountain streams and tickling the sides of trout and bass, that the gray fox runs in a figure eight and the red fox runs in a circle. How to track the bee to the honey hive, where the quail trap caught the most birds, and how curious was the buck deer.

He had eaten with them in their mountain lodge-pole cabins, and they had brought meat to his own family. Their code was the loyalty of the mountain man with all his clannishness, and therefore Lone Watie merited his trust. He was of his kind.

When the War between the States had burst over the nation, the Cherokee naturally sided with the Confederacy against the hated government that had deprived him of his mountain home. Some had joined General Sam Cooper, a few were in the elite brigade of Jo Shelby, but most had followed their leader General Stand Watie, the only Indian General of the Confederacy.

Lone returned to the cabin and squatted before the fire.

"Breakfast," he grunted as he extended the pan of fish to Josey. They ate with their hands while the Indian looked moodily into the fire. "There's been a lot of talk in the settlements. Ye been raising hell in Missouri, they say."

"I reckin," Josey said.

Lone dusted meal on the hearth of the fireplace and from a burlap extracted two cleaned catfish, which he rolled in the meal and placed over the fire.

"Where ye headin'?" he asked.

"Nowheres . . . in pa'ticular," Josey said around a mouthful of fish . . . and then, as if in explanation, "My partner is dead."

For a few harrowing days he had had somewhere to go. It had become an obsession with him, to bring Jamie out of Missouri, to bring him here. With the death of the boy the emptiness came back. As he had

ridden through the night he had caught himself checking back . . . to see to Jamie. The brief purpose was
gone.

Lone Watie asked no questions about the partner,
but he nodded his head in understanding.

"I heard last year thet General Jo Shelby and his
men refused to surrender," Lone said, " . . . heard they
went to Mexico, some kind of fight down there. Ain't
heard nothin' since, but some, I believe, left to join up
with 'em." The Indian spoke flatly, but he shot a quick
glance at Josey to find the effect.

Josey was surprised. "I didn't know there was
other'n thet didn't surrender. I ain't never been farther into Texas than Fannin County. Mexico's a long
way off."

Lone pushed the pan toward Josey. "It is somethin'
to think about," he said. "Men sich as we are . . . our
trade . . . ain't wanted around hereabouts . . . seems
like."

"Something to think about," Josey agreed, and without further ceremony he walked to a willow bed and
unbuckled his guns for the first time in many days.
Placing his hat over his face, he stretched out and was
in deep sleep in a moment. Lone received this un-
spoken confidence with implacable routine.

The days that followed slipped into weeks. There
was no more talk of Mexico . . . but the thought
worked at the mind of Josey. He asked no questions of
Lone, nor did the Indian volunteer information about
himself, but it was apparent that he was in hiding.

As the winter days passed, Josey relaxed his tensions
and even enjoyed helping Lone make fish baskets,
which he did with a skill equaling the Indian's. They
set the baskets in the river with meal balls for bait.
Food was plentiful; besides the fish they ate fat quail

from cunningly set traps on the quail runs, rabbit, and turkey, all seasoned with the wild onion, skunk cabbage, garlic, and herbs Lone dug from the bottoms.

January, 1867, brought snow across the Nations. It swept in a great white storm out of the Cimarron flats, gathered fury over the central plateau, and banked its blanket against the Ozarks. It brought misery to the Plains Indian, the Kiowa, the Comanche, Arapaho, and Pottawatomie . . . short of winter food they were driven toward the settlements. The snow settled in four-foot drifts along the Neosho, but driftwood was plentiful and the cabin was snug. The confinement brought a restlessness to Josey Wales. He had noted the leanness of Lone's provisions. There was no ammunition for his pistol, and the horses were short of grain.

And so it was, as they sat silently around the fire of a bleak evening, Josey placed a fistful of gold pieces in Lone's hand.

"Yankee gold," he said laconically, "we'll be needin' grain . . . ammunition and sich."

Lone stared at the glittering coins in the firelight, and a wolfish smile touched his lips.

"The gold of the enemy, like his corn, is always bright. It'll cause some questions in the settlement, but," he added thoughtfully, "if I tell 'em the blue pony soldiers will take it away from them if they talk . . ."

Bright, crystal-blue days brought the sun's rays in an unseasonable warmth and melted away the snow in a few days and fed new life into the rivulets and streams. Lone brought his gray gelding to the cabin and prepared to leave. Josey carried Lone's saddle to the door, but the Indian shook his head.

"No saddle . . . also no hat . . . no shirt. I'll wear a

blanket and carry only the rifle. I'll be a dumb blanket buck, the soldiers think all Indians with a blanket are too stupid to question."

He left, riding along the river bank, where the marshy bottom would hide his tracks . . . a forlorn, hunched figure under his blanket.

Two days passed, and Josey felt the tenseness of listening for Lone's return. The feeling of the trailed outlaw returned, and the cabin became a trap. On the third day he moved his bedroll and guns to the brush and alternated his watch between river bank and cabin. He could never have been persuaded that Lone would betray him, but many things could have happened.

Lone could have been found out, backtracked by a patrol . . . many of them had Osage trackers. He had moved the roan from the stable and picketed him in the brush when on the afternoon of the fourth day he heard the clear call of the nighthawk. He answered and watched as Lone slipped silently up from the river bank, leading the gray. The Indian looked even more emaciated. Josey suddenly wondered at his age as he saw wrinkles that sagged the bony face. He was older . . . in a dispirited sense that had suckled away the sap from his physical body. As they unloaded the grain and supplies from the back of the horse the Indian said nothing . . . and Josey volunteered no questions.

Around the fireplace they ate a silent meal as both stared into the flames, and then Lone quietly spoke. "There is much talk of ye. Some say ye have killed thirty-five men, some say forty. Ye'll not live long, the soldiers say, for they've raised the price fer yer head. It's five thousand in gold. Many are searching fer ye, and I myself saw five different patrols. I was stopped two times as I returned. I hid the ammunition in the grain."

There was a touch of bitterness in Lone's laugh.

"They would've stolen the grain, but I told them I had gathered it from the leavings of the post . . . thrown out by the white man because it made the white man sick . . . and I was takin' it to my woman. They laughed . . . and said a damn Indian could eat anything. They thought it was poisoned."

Lone fell silent, watching the flames dance along the logs. Josey splattered one of the logs with a long stream of tobacco juice, and after a long time Lone continued. "The trails are patrolled . . . heavy . . . when the weather breaks, they'll begin beatin' the brush. They know ye are in the Nations . . . and they'll find ye."

Josey cut a plug of tobacco. "I reckin," he said easily, with the casual manner of one who had lived for years in the bosom of enemy patrols. He watched the firelight play across the Indian's face. He looked ancient, a haughty and forlorn expression that harked backward toward some wronged god who sat in grieved dignity and disappointment.

"I'm sixty years old," Lone said. "I was a young man with a fine woman and two sons. They died on the Trail of Tears when we left Alabama. Before we were forced to leave, the white man talked of the bad Indian . . . he beat his breast and told why the Indian must leave. Now he's doin' it again. Already the talk is everywhere. The thumpin' of the breast to justify the wrong that will come to the Indian. I have no woman . . . I have no sons. I would not sign the pardon paper. I will not stay and see it again. I would go with ye . . . if ye'll have me."

He had said it all simply, without rancor and with no emotion. But Josey knew what the Indian was saying. He knew of the heartache of lost woman and child . . . of a home that was no more. And he knew that Lone Watie, the Cherokee, in saying simply that he would go with him . . . meant much more . . . that he had chosen Josey as his people . . . a like warrior with a common cause, a common suffrage . . . a respect for courage. And as it was with such men as Josey Wales, he could not show these things he felt. Instead, he said, "They're payin' to see me dead. Ye could do a lot better by driftin' south on yer own."

Now he knew why Lone had refused to sign the pardon paper . . . why he had deliberately made an outcast of himself, hoping that the blame would be placed on such men as himself . . . rather than his people. On this trip he had become convinced that nothing would save the Nation of the Cherokee.

Lone took his gaze from the fire and looked across the hearth into the eyes of Josey. He spoke slowly. "It is good that a man's enemies want him dead, for it proves he has lived a life of worth. I am old but I will ride free as long as I live. I would ride with such a man."

Josey reached into a paper sack Lone had brought back with the supplies and drew forth a round ball of red, hard rock candy. He held it up to the light. "Jest like a damn Indian," he said, "always buying somethin' red, meant fer foolishness."

Lone's smile broadened into a deep-throated chuckle of relief. He knew he would ride with Josey Wales.

The bitterness of February slipped toward March as they made preparation for the trail. Grass would be greening farther south, and the longhorn herds, moving up from Texas on the Shawnee Trail for Sedalia, would hide their own movements south.

Mexico! The thought had lingered in Josey's mind. Once, wintering at Mineral Creek, an old Confederate cavalryman of General McCulloch's had visited their campfires, regaling the guerrillas with stories of his soldiering with General Zachary Taylor at Monterrey in 1847. He told tales of fiestas and balmy fragrant nights, of dancing and Spanish *señoritas*. There had been the thrilling recital of when the emissary of General Santa Anna had come down to inform Taylor that he was surrounded by twenty thousand troops and must surrender. How the Mexican military band, in the early morning light, had played the "Dequela," the no-quarter song, as the thousands of pennants fluttered in the breeze from the hills surrounding Taylor's men. And Old Zack had ridden down the line, mounted on "Whitey," bellering, "Double-shot yer guns and give 'em hell, damn 'em."

The stories had enthralled the Missouri pistol fighters, farm boys who had found nothing of the romantic in their dirty Border War. Josey had remembered the interlude around that Texas campfire. If a feller had nowheres in pa'ticlar to ride . . . well, why not Mexico!

They saddled up on a raw March morning. An icy wind sent showers of frost from the tree branches, and the ground was still frozen before dawn. The horses, grain-slick and eager, fought the bits in their mouths and crow-hopped against the saddles. Josey left the heading to Lone, and the Indian led away from the cabin, following the bank of the Neosho. Neither of them looked back.

Lone had discarded the blanket. The gray cavalry hat shaded his eyes. Around his waist he wore the

Colts' pistol, belted low. If he would ride with Josey Wales . . . then he would ride as boldly . . . for what he was . . . a companion Rebel. Only the hawk-bronze face, the plaited hair that dangled to his shoulders . . . the boot moccasins . . . marked him as Indian.

Their progress was slow. Traveling dim trails, often where no trail showed at all, they stayed with the crooks and turns of the river as it threaded south through the Cherokee Nation. The third day of riding found them just north of Fort Gibson, and they were forced to leave the river to circle that Army post. They did so at night, striking the Shawnee Trail and fording the Arkansas. At dawn they were out on rolling prairie and in the Creek Indian Nation.

It was nearing noon when the gelding pulled up lame. Lone dismounted and ran his hands around the leg, down to the hoof. The horse jumped as he pressed a tendon. "Pulled," he said, "too much damn stable time."

Josey scanned the horizon about them . . . there were no riders in sight, but they were exposed, with only one horse, and the humps in the prairie had a way of suddenly disclosing what had not been there a moment before. Josey swung a leg around the saddle horn and looked thoughtfully at the gelding. "Thet hoss won't ride fer a week."

Lone nodded gloomily. His face was a mask, but his heart sank. It was only right that he stay behind . . . he could not endanger Josey Wales.

Josey cut a wad of tobacco. "How fer to thet tradin' post on the Canadian?"

Lone straightened. "Four . . . maybe six mile. That would be Zukie Limmer's post . . . but patrols are comin' and goin' around there, Creek Indian police too."

Josey swung his foot into the stirrup. "They all ride hosses, and a hoss is what we need. Wait here." He jumped the roan into a run. As he topped a rise he looked back. Lone was on foot, running behind him, leading the limping gelding.

9

The trading post was set back a mile from the Canadian on a barren flat of shale rock and brush. It was a one-story log structure that showed no sign of human life except the thin column of smoke that rose from a chimney. Behind the post was a half-rotted barn, obviously past use. Back of the barn a pole corral held horses.

From his position on the rise Josey counted the horses . . . thirty of them . . . but there were no saddles in sight . . . no harness. That meant trade horses . . . somebody had made a trade. For several minutes he watched. The hitch rack before the post was empty, and he could see no sign of movement anywhere in his range of vision. He eased the roan down the hill and circled the corral. Before he was halfway around, he saw the horse he wanted, a big black with deep chest and rounded barrel . . . nearly as big as his roan. He rode to the front of the post, and looping the reins of the roan on the hitch rack, strode to the heavy front door.

Zukie Limmer was nervous and frightened. He had reason. He held his trading post contract under auspices of the U.S. Army, which specifically forbade the sale of liquor. Zukie made more profit from his bootlegging than he did from all his trade goods cheating of the Creeks. Now he was frightened. The two men had brought the horses in yesterday and were waiting, they said, for the Army detachment from Fort Gibson to come and inspect them for buying. They had turned their own horses into the corral, and dragging their saddles and gear into the post, had slept on the dirt floor without so much as asking a leave to do so. He knew them only as Yoke and Al, but he knew they were dangerous, for they had about them the leering smiles of thinly disguised threat as they took whatever pleased them with the remark, "Put that on our bill," at which they both invariably burst into roars of laughter at a seemingly obvious joke. They claimed to have papers on the horses, but Zukie suspected the horse herd to be Comanch . . . the fruits of a Comanche raiding party on Texas ranches of the Southwest.

The evening before, the larger of the two, Yoke, had thrown a huge arm around the narrow shoulders of Zukie, drawing him close in an overbearing, confidential manner. He had blown the breath of his rotten teeth into Zukie's face while he assured him, "We got papers on them horses . . . good papers. Ain't we, Al?"

He had winked broadly at Al, and both had laughed uproariously. Zukie had scuttled back behind the heavy plank set on barrels that served as his bar. During the night he had moved his gold box back into the sloping lean-to shed where he slept. All day he had stayed behind the plank, first hoping for the Army patrol . . . now dreading it; for the men had broken into his whiskey barrel and had been liquoring up since midmorning.

Once, Zukie had almost forgotten his fear. When the Indian woman had brought out the noon meal and placed the beef platters before them on the rough table, they had grabbed her. She had stood passively while they ran rough hands over her thighs and buttocks and made obscene suggestions to each other.

"How much you take fer this squaw?" Al, the ferret-looking one, had asked as he stroked the woman's stomach.

"She ain't fer sale," Zukie had snapped . . . then, alarmed at his own brevity, a whine entered his tone . . . "That is . . . she ain't mine . . . I mean, she works here."

Yoke had winked knowingly at Al, "He could put 'er on the bill, Al." They had laughed at the remark until Yoke fell off the stool. The woman had escaped back into the kitchen.

Zukie was not outraged at their treatment of the woman; it was that he had anticipated her for himself. She had been there at the post just four days, and as was his way, Zukie Limmer never entered upon anything in a straight manner . . . he sidled his way, crablike, forward. Cunning was his nature; it made the prize better.

She had walked into the post from the west and had offered an old dirty blanket for sale. Zukie had sized her up immediately. She was an outcast. The heavy scar running the length of her right nostril was the

punishment of some of the Plains tribes for unfaithful-
ness. "One too many bucks," Zukie had snickered and
repeated it. It was clever, and Zukie savored his humor.
She was not unpretty. Maybe twenty-five or thirty,
still slender, with pointed breasts and rounded thighs
that pushed against the fringed doeskin. Her moccasins had been worn through and hung in tatters on
swollen feet. Her bronze face, framed by plaited black
hair, was stoical, but her eyes reflected the haunted
look of a hurt animal.

Zukie had felt the saliva juices entering his mouth as
he looked at her. He had run his hands over the firm
roundness of her breasts and she had not moved. She
was hungry . . . and helpless. He had put her to work
. . . and he knew how to train Indians . . . especially
Indian women. He had watched for the opportunity,
and when she had fallen and overturned a nearly
empty barrel of brine he had pushed her face into the
floor with one hand while he had beaten her with a
barrel stave until his arm was weary. She had stayed
motionless under the beating, but he had felt the animal strength in her. Sinewy, flat stomach, firm buttocks and thighs . . . properly mastered; Zukie relished
the thought. When he ate at his table he opened the
back door of the lean-to and made the woman squat
outside, with the half-starved hound, and he had tossed
scraps to her to eat. She was about ready to be moved
into his bed, and she wouldn't be uppity.

Now Yoke demanded more food, and the Indian
woman came, bringing more beef and potatoes. As she
reached the table Yoke encircled her waist with a big
arm, lifted her from the floor, and slammed her length-
wise on the tabletop. He pressed his huge body down
on her breasts, and grabbing her hair, tried to hold her
upturned face steady while he slobbered over her

mouth. His voice was thick with lust and liquor. "We're gonna have us a little squaw . . . ain't we, Al?"

Al was caressing the thighs of the woman, his hands moved under her doeskin skirt. She kicked and twisted her face, not crying out . . . but she was helpless. The heavy door opened suddenly, and Josey Wales stepped through. Everybody froze in motion.

Zukie Limmer knew it was Josey Wales. The talk of the reward was everywhere. The description of the man was exact; the twin tied-down .44's, the buckskin jacket, the gray cavalry hat . . . the heavy white scar that jagged the cheeks. The man must be crazy! No, he must not care whether he lives or dies, to go about making no attempt to disguise himself.

Zukie had heard the stories of the outlaw. No man could feel safe in his presence, and Zukie felt the recklessness . . . the ruthlessness that emanated from the man. The threat of Yoke and Al faded as of naughty schoolboys. Zukie Limmer placed his hands on the plank . . . in plain sight . . . and a cold, dread fear convinced him his life hung balanced on the whim of this killer.

Josey Wales moved with a practiced quickness out of the door's silhouette and with the same fluid motion moved to the end of the bar so that he faced the door. He appeared not to notice the Indian woman and her tormentors. They still held her but watched, fascinated, as he leaned easily on the bar. Zukie turned to face him . . . keeping his hands tightly on the plank . . . and looked into black eyes that were cold and flat . . . and he physically shivered. Josey smiled. Perhaps it was meant to be friendly, but the smile only served to deepen and whiten the big scar so that his face took on an inexpressible cruelty. Zukie felt like a mouse before a big purring cat and so was impelled to make some offer.

"Have a whiskey, mister?" he heard himself squeaking.

Josey waited a long time. "Reckin not," he said dryly.

"I got some cold beer . . . good brewed-up Choc. It's . . . it's on the house," Zukie stammered.

Josey eased the hat back on his head. "Well now, that's right neighborly of ye, friend."

Zukie placed a huge tin cup before him and from a barrel dippered the dark liquid into it. He was encouraged by the action of Josey Wales drinking beer. It was, after all, a human act. Perhaps the man had some reasonable qualities about him. Surely he could think humanely . . . and sociably.

Josey wiped the beer from his mustache with the back of a hand. "Matter of fact," he said, "I'm lookin' to buy a hoss."

"A hoss . . . ah . . . a horse?" Zukie repeated stupidly.

Al had staggered to the bar. "Gimme a bucket of that Choc," he said thickly.

Zukie, still staring at Josey, dipped a tin bucket of the beer from the barrel and placed it on the bar. "The horses," he said, "belong to these gentlemen. They'll more than likely. . . that is . . . I'm sure they'll sell you one."

Al turned slowly to face Josey, holding the bucket of beer waist-high, and under it he held a pistol . . . the hammer already thumbed back. A sly, triumphant smile wreathed his face.

"Josey Wales," he breathed . . . and then chortled, "Josey Wales, by God! Five thousand gold simoleons walkin' right in. Mr. Chain Blue Lightening hisself, that ever'body's so scairt of. Well now, Mr. Lighten-

ing, you move a hair, twitch a finger . . . and I'll
splatter yore guts agin the wall. Come over here,
Yoke," he called aside to his partner.

Yoke shuffled forward, loosing the Indian woman.
Zukie was terrified as he looked from Al to Josey. The
outlaw was staring steadily into the eyes of Al . . . he
hadn't moved. Confidence began to return to Zukie.

"Now look, Al," Zukie whined, "the man is in my
place. I recognized him, and I'm due a even split. I . . ."

"Shet up," Al said viciously, without taking his eyes
from Josey, "shet up, you goddamned nanny goat. I'm
the one that got 'em."

Al was growing nervous from the strain. "Now," he
said testily, "when I tell you to move, Mr. Lightening,
you move slow, like 'lasses in the wintertime, or I drop
the hammer. You ease yore hands down, take them
guns out, butt first, and hold 'em out so Yoke can git
'em. You understand? Nod, damn you."

Josey nodded his head.

"Now," Al instructed, "ease the pistols out."

With painful slowness Josey pulled the Colts and
extended them butt first toward Yoke. A finger of each
hand was in the trigger guard. Yoke stepped forward
and reached for the proffered handles. His hands were
almost on the butts of the pistols when they spun on
the fingers of Josey with the slightest flick of his wrists.
As if by magic the pistols were reversed, barrels pointing at Al and Yoke . . . but Al never saw it.

The big right-hand .44 exploded with an ear split-
ting roar that lifted Al from the floor and arched his
body backward. Yoke was dumbfounded. A full second ticked by before he clawed for the pistol at his
hip. He knew he was making a futile effort, but he
read death in the black eyes of Josey Wales. The left-

hand Colt boomed, and the top of Yoke's head . . . and most of his brains . . . were splattered against a post.

"My God!" Zukie screamed. "My God!" And he sank sobbing to the floor. He had witnessed the pistol spin. A few years later the Texas gunfighter John Wesley Hardin would execute the same trick to disarm Wild Bill Hickok in Abilene. It would become known in the West as the "Border Roll," in honor of the Missouri Border pistol fighters who had invented it . . . but few would dare practice it, for it required a master pistol-eer.

Acrid blue smoke filled the room. The Indian woman had not moved, nor did she now, but her eyes followed Josey Wales.

"Stand up, mister," Josey leaned over the plank and looked down at Zukie, who pulled himself to his feet. His hands were trembling as he watched the outlaw carefully cut a chew of tobacco and return the twist to his jacket. He chewed for a moment, looking thoughtfully at Zukie.

"Now, let's see," he said with studied contemplation, "ye say them hosses belong to these here pilgrims?" He designated the "pilgrims" by accurately hitting Al's up-turned face with a stream of tobacco juice.

"Yes . . . Yes," Zukie was eagerly helpful, " . . . and Mr. Wales, I was only trying to throw them off . . . to help you . . . with that talk of the reward."

"I 'preciate thet kindly," Josey said dryly, "but gittin' back to the hosses, 'pears like these here pore pilgrims won't be in the need of them hosses no more . . . seein' as how they have passed on . . . so I reckin the hosses is more or less public property . . . wouldn't ye say?"

Zukie nodded vigorously, "Yes, I would say that . . . I would agree to that. It sounds fair and right to me."

"Fair'n fair and right as rain," Josey said with satisfaction. "Now me being a public citizen and sich as that," Josey continued, "I reckin I'll take along my part of the propitty, not havin' time to wait around fer the court to divide it all up."

"I think you should have all the horses," Zukie said generously. "They . . . that is, they really belong to you."

"I ain't a hawg," Josey said. "We got to think of the other public citizens. One hoss will do me fine. You git thet loop of rope hangin' yonder, and ye come on out, and we'll ketch up my propitty."

Zukie scurried out the door ahead of Josey and trotted to the corral. They caught up the big black. Josey rigged a halter and mounted the roan. From his saddle he looked down at Zukie, who nervously shifted his feet.

"Reckin ye can live, mister," and his voice was cold, "but a woman is a woman. I got friends in the Nations, and word gittin' to me of thet woman bein' mistreated would strike me unkindly."

Zukie bobbed his head, "I pledge to you, Mr. Wales . . . I give my solemn word, she will not be . . . again. I will . . ."

"I'll be seein' ye," and with that, Josey sank spurs to the roan and was off in a whirl of dust, leading the black behind him. The Indian woman watched him from where she crouched behind the lean-to.

As Josey topped the first rise he found Lone waiting with rifle trained on the trading post. Lone's eyes glistened as he looked at the black.

"A feller would have to sleep with thet hoss to keep his grandma from stealing him," he said admiringly.

"Yeah," Josey grinned. "Got him cheap too. But if

we ain't movin' on in a minute, the Army's most like to git 'em. A patrol is due any minute from Fort Gibson."

They worked fast, switching Lone's gear from the gray gelding to the black. The gelding moved off immediately, cropping grass.

"He'll be all right in a week . . . maybe he'll run free the rest of his life," Lone said wistfully.

"Let's move out," Josey said, and he swung the big roan down the hill, followed by Lone on the black. They were magnificently mounted now; the roan scarcely a hand higher than the strong black horse. Fording the Canadian, they moved toward the Seminole and the Choctaw Nations.

Less than an hour later, Zukie Limmer was pouring out his story to the Army patrol from Fort Gibson, and in three hours dispatches were alerting the state of Texas. Added to the dispatches were these words: SHOOT ON SIGHT. DO NOT ATTEMPT TO DISARM, REPEAT: DO NOT ATTEMPT TO DISARM. FIVE THOUSAND DOLLARS REWARD: DEAD.

The tale of the pistol spin fled southward, keeping pace with the dispatches. The story grew with each telling through the campfires of the drovers coming up the trail . . . and spread to the settlements. Violent Texas knew and talked of Josey Wales long before he was to reach her borders . . . the bloody ex-lieutenant of Bloody Bill; the pistol fighter with the lightning hands and stone nerves who mastered the macabre art of death from the barrels of Colt .44's.

10

They rode far into the night. Josey left the trail heading to Lone and followed his lead. The Cherokee was a crafty trailsman, and with the threat of pursuit he brought all his craft into practice.

Once, for a mile, they rode down the middle of a shallow creek and brought their horses to the bank when Lone found loose shale rock that carried no print. For a distance of ten miles they boldly traveled the well-marked Shawnee Trail, mixing their tracks with the tracks of the trail. Each time they paused to rest the horses Lone drove a stick in the ground . . . grasping it with his teeth, he "listened," feeling for the vibrations of horses. Each time as he remounted he shook his head in puzzlement, "Very light sound . . . maybe one horse . . . but it's stayin' with us . . . we ain't shakin' it off."

Josey frowned, "I don't figger one hoss . . . maybe it's a damn buffalo . . . 'er a wild hoss follerin'."

It was after midnight when they rested. Rolled in blankets on the bank of a creek that meandered toward Pine Mountain, they slept with bridle reins wrapped about their wrists. They grained the horses but left the saddles on them, loosely cinched.

Up before dawn, they made a cold breakfast of jerky beef and biscuits and double-grained the horses for the hard riding. Lone suddenly placed his hand on the ground. He kneeled with ear pressed against the earth.

"It's a horse," he said quietly, "comin' down the creek." Now Josey could hear it crashing through the undergrowth. He tied the horses back behind a persimmon tree and stepped into the small clearing.

"I'll be bait man," he said calmly. Lone nodded and slipped the big knife from its scabbard. He placed it between his teeth and slid noiselessly into the brush toward the creek. Now Josey could see the horse. It was a spotted paint, and the rider was leaning from its back, studying the ground as he rode. Now he saw Josey but didn't pause, but instead lifted the paint into a trot. The horse was within twenty yards of Josey and he could see that the rider wore a heavy blanket over his head, falling around his shoulders.

Suddenly a figure leaped from the brush astride the paint and toppled the rider from the horse. It was Lone. He was over the rider, lying on the ground, and raised his knife for the downward death stroke. "Wait!" Josey shouted.

The blanket had fallen away from the rider. It was the Indian woman. Lone sat down on her in amazement. A vicious-looking hound was attacking one of his moccasined feet, and he kicked at the dog as he rose. The Indian woman calmly brushed her skirt and stood up. As Josey approached she pointed back up the creek.

"Pony soldiers," she said, "two hours." Lone stared at her.

"How in hell . . . " he said.

"She was at the trading post," Josey said, then to the woman, "How many pony soldiers?"

She shook her head, and Josey turned to Lone. "Ask her about the pony soldiers . . . try some kind of lingo."

"Sign," Lone said. "All Indians know sign talk, even tribes that cain't understand each other's spoke word."

He moved his hands and fingers through the air. The woman nodded vigorously and answered with her own hands.

"She says," Lone turned to Josey, "there are twenty pony soldiers, two . . . maybe three hours back . . . wait, she's talkin' agin."

The Indian woman's hands moved rapidly for a space of several minutes while Lone watched. He chuckled . . . laughed . . . then fell silent.

"What is it?" Josey asked. "Hell, man, cain't ye shet her up?"

Lone held his palm forward toward the woman and looked admiringly at Josey.

"She told me of the fight in the tradin' post . . . of your magic guns. She says ye are a great warrior and a great man. She is Cheyenne. Thet sign she give of cuttin' the wrist . . . thet's the sign of the Cheyenne . . . every Plains tribe has a sign that identifies them. The movin' of her hand forward, wigglin', is the sign of the snake . . . the Comanche sign. She said the two men ye killed were traders with the Comanch . . . called Comancheros . . . 'them that deals with Comanch.' She said she was violated by a buck of the Arapaho . . . their

sign is the 'dirty nose' sign . . . when she held her nose
with her fingers . . . and that the Cheyenne Chief,
Moke-to-ve-to, or Black Kettle, believed she did not
resist enough . . . she should have killed herself . . . so
she was whupped, had her nose slit, and was cast out
to die." Lone paused. "Her name, by the way, is Taketoha . . . means 'Little Moonlight'."

"She can shore talk," Josey said admiringly. He spat
tobacco juice at the dog . . . and the hound snarled.
"Tell her," Josey said, "to go back to the tradin' post.
She will be treated better now. Tell her that many
men want to kill us . . . that we gotta ride fast . . . thet
there's too much danger fer a woman," Josey paused,
"and tell her we 'preciate what she's done fer us."

Lone's hands moved rapidly again. He watched her
solemnly as she answered. Finally he looked at Josey,
and there was the pride of the Indian when he spoke.
"She says she cannot go back. That she stole a rifle,
supplies, and the hoss. She says she would not go back
if she could . . . that she will foller in our tracks. Ye
saved her life. She says she can cook, track, and fight.
Our ways are her ways. She says she ain't got nowheres else to go." Lone's face was expressionless, but
his eyes looked askance at Josey. "She's shore pretty,"
he added with hopeful recommendation.

Josey spat, "Damn all conniption hell. Here we go,
trailin' into Texas like a waggin train. Well . . . " he
sighed as he turned to the horses, "she'll jest have to
track if she falls back, and when she gits tired she can
quit."

As they swung into their saddles Lone said, "She
thinks I'm a Cherokee Chief."

"I wonder where she got thet idee," Josey remarked
dryly. Little Moonlight picked up her rifle and blanket
and swung expertly astride the paint. She waited

humbly, eyes cast to the ground, for the men to take the trail.

"I wonder," Josey said as they walked the horses out of the brush.

"Wonder what?" Lone asked.

"I was jest wonderin'," he said, "I reckin that mangy red-bone hound ain't got nowheres to go neither."

Lone laughed and led the way, followed closely by Josey. At a respectful distance the blanketed Little Moonlight rode the paint, and at her heels the bony hound sniffed the trail.

They traveled south, then southwest, skirting Pine Mountain on their left and keeping generally to open prairie. More grass showed now on the land. Lone kept the black at a ground-eating canter, and the big roan easily stayed with him, but Little Moonlight fell farther and farther behind. By midafternoon Josey could just make out her bobbing head as she pushed the rough-riding paint nearly a mile behind. The soldiers had not come into sight, but late in the afternoon a party of half-naked Indians armed with rifles rode over a rise to their left and brought their ponies at an angle to intercept them.

Lone slowed the black.

"I count twelve," Josey said as he rode alongside.

Lone nodded. "They are Choctaws, riding down to meet the trail herds. They will ask payment fer crossing their lands . . . then they will cut out cattle . . . permission or not."

The Indians rode closer, but after they had inspected the two heavily armed men on the big horses . . . they veered off and slackened pace. They had ridden on for another quarter mile when Lone slid the black to a halt so suddenly that Josey almost ran his mount over him.

"Taketoha!" he shouted, "Little Moon . . . !" Simultaneously, they whirled their horses and set them running back over the trail. Coming to a rise they saw the Indians riding close, but not too close, to the paint horse. Little Moonlight was holding the rifle steady, and with it she swept the squad of Indians. The Choctaws saw Lone and Josey waiting on the rise and turned away from the Indian woman. They had gotten the message; that the squaw was, somehow, a member of this strange caravan that included two hard-appearing riders mounted on giant horses and a cadaverous-looking hound with long ears and bony flanks.

It was midnight when they camped on the banks of Clear Boggy Creek, less than a day's ride from the Red River and Texas. An hour later Little Moonlight jogged into camp on the paint.

Josey heard her slip silently around their blankets. He saw Lone rise and give grain to the paint. She rolled in a blanket a little distance from them and did not eat before she slept.

Her movements woke Josey before dawn, and he smelled cooking but saw no fire. Little Moonlight had dragged a hollow log close to them, carved a hole in its side, and placed a black pot over a captive, hidden fire.

Lone was already eating. "I'm gonna take up tepee livin' . . . if it's like this," he grinned. And as Josey stepped to feed the horses Lone said, "She's already grained 'em . . . and watered 'em . . . and rubbed 'em down . . . and cinched the saddles. Might as well set yore bottom down like a chief and eat."

Josey took a bowl from her and sat cross-legged by the log. "I see the Cherokee Chief is already eatin'," he said.

"Cherokee Chiefs have big appetites," Lone

grinned, belched, and stretched. The hound growled at the movement . . . he was chewing on a mangled rabbit. Josey watched the dog as he ate.

"I see ol' hound gits his own," he said. "Re'clects me of a red-bone we had back home in Tennessee. I went with Pa to tradin'. They had pretty blue ticks, julys, and sich, but Pa, he paid fifty cent and a jug o' white fer a old red-bone that had a broke tail, one eye out, and half a ear bit off. I ast Pa why, and he said minute he saw that ol' hound, he knowed he had sand . . . thet he'd been there and knowed what it was all about . . . made the best 'coon hound we ever had."

Lone looked at Little Moonlight as she packed gear on the paint. "It is so . . . and many times . . . with women. Yore Pa was a knowin' mountain man."

The wind held a smell of moist April as they rode south, still in the Choctaw Nation. At dusk they sighted the Red River, and by full dark the three of them had forded not far from the Shawnee Trail. They set foot on the violent ground of Texas.

11

Texas in 1867 was in the iron grip of the Union General Phil Sheridan's military rule. He had removed Governor James W. Throckmorton from office and appointed his own Governor, E. M. Pease. Pease, a figurehead for the Northern Army under orders of radical politicians in Washington, would soon be succeeded by another Military Governor, E. J. Davis, but the conditions would remain the same.

Only those who took the "ironclad oath" could vote. Union soldiers stood in long lines at every ballot box. All Southern sympathizers had been thrown out of office. Judges, mayors, sheriffs were replaced by what Texans called "scalawags," if the turncoats were from the South, and "carpetbaggers," if they were from the North. Armed, blue-coated Militia, called "Regula-

tors," imposed . . . or tried to . . . the will of the
Governor, and mobs of Union Leaguers, half-controlled
by the politicians, settled like locusts over the land.

The effects of the vulturous greed and manipula-
tions of the politicians were everywhere, as they sought
to confiscate property and home and line their pockets
from levy and tax. The Regular Army, as usual, was
caught in the middle and in the main stood aside or
devoted their efforts to the often futile task of attempting to contain the raids of the bloody Comanche and
Kiowa that encroached even into central Texas. These
Tartars of the Plains were ferociously defending their
last free domain that stretched from deep in Mexico to
the Cimarron in the north.

The names of untamed Rebels were gaining bloody
prominence; Cullen Baker, the heller from Louisiana,
was becoming widely known. Captain Bob Lee, who
had served under the incomparable Bedford Forrest in
Tennessee, was waging a small war with the Union
Leaguers headed by Lewis Peacock. Operating out of
Fannin, Collins, and Hunt counties, Lee was setting
northeast Texas aflame. There was already a price on
his head. Bill Longley, the cold killer from Evergreen,
was a wanted man, and farther south, around DeWitt
and Gonzales counties, there was the Taylor clan.
Headed by the ex-Confederate Captain Creed Taylor,
there were brothers Josiah, Rufus, Pitkin, William, and
Charlie . . . with sons Buck, Jim, and a whole army of
a second generation.

Out of the Carolinas, Georgia, and Alabama, they
fought under the orders of the Taylor family motto,
marrowed in their blood from birth, "Whoever sheds a
Taylor's blood, by a Taylor's hand must die." And they
meant it. Entire towns were terrorized in the shoot-

outs between the Taylors, their kith and kin . . . and the Regulators headed by Bill Sutton and his entourage. They were tough and mean; stubborn to defend their "propitty"; they had never been whupped, and they aimed to prove it.

Simp Dixon, a Taylor kinsman, died at Cotton Gin, Texas, his back to a wall . . . weighted down with lead . . . and both .44's blazing. He took five Regulators with him. The Clements brothers went "helling" through the carpetbag-controlled towns and periodically rode up the trail when the Texas heat got too unhealthy. The untended ranches of four years had loosed thousands of wild longhorns in the brush. The Northeast needed beef, and the Southern riders filled the trails as they "brush-popped" the cattle into herds and angled them north.

First up the Shawnee to Sedalia, Missouri . . . then the Chisholm to Abilene, Kansas . . . the Western Trail to Dodge City, as the rail lines moved west. Each spring and fall they turned the railhead cattle towns into "Little Texas" and brought a brand of wildness that forevermore would stamp the little villages in history.

It would be a year before a young lad, John Wesley Hardin, would begin his fantastically bloody career . . . but he would be only one of many. General Sherman said of the time and the place, "If I owned Texas and Hell, I would rent out Texas and live in Hell." Well, Sherman knowed where his fit company was at. For Texans . . . them as couldn't fork the bronc had best move out, preferably in a pine box.

And now word flew down the Trail. The Missouri Rebel and unequaled pistol fighter, Josey Wales, was Texas bound. It was enough to make a Texan stomp the ground in glee and spit into the wind. For the politician it brought frantic thoughts and feverish action. Both sides braced for the coming.

Campfires twinkled as far as the eye could see. Early herds, pushing for the top market dollar after a winter's beef-hungry span in the North, were stacked almost end to end. Longhorns bawled and scuffled as cowboys rounded them into a settling for the night. Josey, Lone, and Little Moonlight . . . riding close now . . . passed near the lead campfires, out of the light. The *plink-plank* of a five-string banjo sounded tinny against the cattle sounds, and a mournful voice rose in song:

> "They say I cain't take up my rifle
> and fight 'em now nor more,
> But I ain't a'gonna love 'em
> Now thet is certain shore.
> And I don't want no pardon
> Fer whut I was and am,
> And I won't be reconstructed,
> And I don't give a damn."

They dry-camped in a shallow gully, away from the herds. Unable to picket-graze the horses and with the added appetite of the paint horse, the grain was running low.

It was chuck time for the cowboys of the Gatling brothers' trail herd. There were three Gatling brothers and eleven riders pushing three thousand head of longhorns. It had been a rough day. Herds were strung out behind them, and immediately on their heels Mexican vaqueros with a smaller herd had pushed and shouted at them for more speed. Several fights had broken out through the day, and the riders were in an ugly mood. The longhorns were not yet "trail-broke," still wild as they were driven from the brush; and they had made charges, all day long, away from the main body, which had kept the cowboys busy. Ten of them squatted now, or sat cross-legged around the fire, wolfing beans and beef. Half their number would have to relieve the riders circling the herd and take up first night watch. They were in no hurry to climb back in the saddle. Rough-garbed, most of them wore the chapparal leather guards . . . the cowboys called them "chaps" . . . and heavy pistols hung from sagging belts about their waists.

The voice came clear, "Haaallooo, the camp." Every man stiffened. Four of them faded a few paces back from the fire into the darkness. They had "papers" on them, and though they were protected by the code of the trail . . . every rider of the trail herd would fight to the death in their defense . . . there was no sense borrern' trouble from a nosey lawman.

The trail boss, for a long moment, continued chewing his beef, giving them as needed it "scarcin' time." Then he stood up and bawled, "Come on in!" They heard the horse walking slowly . . . then into the firelight. It was a huge black that snorted and skittered as the rider brought him close. He swung down and did not trust the black to rein-stand but tied him to the wheel of the chuck wagon. Without another word, he brought his tin plate and cup from a saddlebag, dipped huge portions of bean and beef from the pot, calmly poured black coffee into the cup, and squatted, eating, in the circle of riders. It was the custom. The chuck was open claim to any rider on the trail.

It was a fractious practice to ask questions in Texas. Whenever a man asked one, it was invariably preceded by "no offense meant" . . . unless, of course, he did mean offense . . . in which case he prepared to draw his pistol. There was no need for questions anyhow. Every cowboy present could "read." The rider wore moccasin boots, the long, plaited black hair. He was Indian. The gray cavalry hat meant Confederate. Confederate Cherokee. There was the tied-down .44 and knife. A fightin' man. He came from the Nations, to the north, and he was riding south . . . otherwise, if he had come from the south, he'd have chucked at the hind-end herd. The horse was too good for a regular Indian or cowboy, therefore he was on a fast run from somethin' when a feller had to have the best in horseflesh. The "reading" required only a minute. They approved . . . and gave evidence of their approval by resuming their conversations.

"Onliest way they'll ever git Wales is from the back," a bearded cowpuncher opined as he sopped his beans with a biscuit.

Another rose and refilled his plate. "Whit rode with Bill Todd and Fletch Taylor in Missouri . . . he says he seen Wales oncet in '65, at Baxter Springs. Drawed on three Redlegs. . . . Whit says ye couldn't see his hands move . . . and na'ar Redleg cleared leather."

"Bluebellies cut his trail in the Nations," another said. "Say thar's another rider . . . maybe two with 'em now."

The trail boss spoke, "He was knowed to have friends 'mongst the Cherokees. . . . " His voice trailed off . . . he had spoken before he thought . . . and now there was an awkward silence. Eyes cut furtively toward the Indian, who appeared not to have heard. He was busying himself over his tin plate.

The trail boss cleared his throat and addressed himself to the Indian, "Stranger, we was wonderin' about trail conditions to the north. That is, if ye come from that d'rection, no offense."

Lone looked up casually and spoke around a mouthful of beef. "None taken," he said. "Grazin' ought to be good. Day t'other side of the Red, ye'll be pestered by Choctaws . . . little bunches of 'em, old rifles, muzzle load. Canadian ain't up . . . leastwise, it wa'ant few days ago. If ye're branchin' off on the Chisholm, ye'll strike the Arkansas west of the Neosho . . . ought not be runnin' high . . . but I never crossed that fer west. East, on the Shawnee . . . she's up a mite." He sopped the remains of the beans, washed his tin plate with sand, and downed the last of the coffee. "Lookin' to buy a little stock grain . . . iff'n ye got it to spare."

"We're grazin' our remuda . . . ain't totin' no grain," the trail boss said, "but fer jest the one hoss, mebbe. . ."

"Three hosses," Lone said.

The trail boss turned to the cook, "Give 'em the oats in the chuck," and to Lone, "Ain't much . . . no more'n fer a day 'er two . . . but we can eat corn fritters . . . cain't we, boys?"

The cowboys nodded their big hats in unison. They knew.

"I'd be obliged to pay," Lone said as he accepted the sack of oats from the cook.

"Not likely," a cowboy spoke clear and loud from the fire.

As Lone swung up on the black, the trail boss held his bridle briefly, "Union Leaguers, twenty-five . . . thirty of 'em . . . combed through the herds a day's ride back . . . headed west. Heerd tell Regulators was poppin' brush all through this here neck o' country." He loosed his hands from the bridle.

Lone looked down at the trail boss, and his eyes

glittered. "Obliged," he said quietly, whirled the black, and was gone.

"Good luck," the voices floated to him from the campfire.

Josey and Little Moonlight had waited in the shallow wash. He sat, holding the horses' reins, and Little Moonlight stood behind him, high on the bank, and watched for Lone's return. Before he heard Lone's approach, she touched him on the arm. "Hoss," she said.

Josey smiled in the dark, a Cheyenne squaw, talkin' like a leather-popper. He listened to Lone's report in silence. Somehow . . . he had taken it for granted . . . that Texas would be as it was when he had wintered here during the War; everything peaceful behind the Confederate lines . . . but now, the same treacheries were present that had plagued Missouri all the many long years.

His face hardened. It would be no leisurely ride to Mexico. He was surprised that his name was so well known, and the term "Regulators" was new to him. Lone watched and waited patiently for Josey to speak. Lone Watie was an expert trailsman. He had been a cavalryman of the first order, but he knew by instinct that this climate of Texas required the leadership of the master guerrilla.

"We'll night-ride," Josey said grimly, "lay out in the washes and tree cover by day. Farther south we git, better off we ought to be. Let's ride." They pointed the tired horses south, giving wide berth to the fires of the trail herds.

By the morning of the fourth day they sighted the Brazos and camped in a thick scope of cottonwoods a half mile back from the Towash road. Little Moonlight curled at the base of a tree and instantly was asleep.

There was no more horse grain, and Lone rope-picketed the horses on the sparse grass . . . and lay sprawled on the ground, his hat covering his face.

Josey Wales watched the Towash road. From where he sat, back to a cottonwood, he could see riders as they passed below him. A lot of riders, singly and in groups. Occasionally a wagon feathering up the powder-gray dust . . . and here and there a fancy hack. Toward the west he could see the town only dimly visible in the dust haze and a racetrack at the edge. Racing day; that meant a lot of people. Sometimes you could move 'mongst a lot of people and bear no notice at all.

Josey worked at a heavy tobacco cud and mused his thinking toward a plan. He saw no blue riders on the road. Mexico, that temporary goal for temporary men who had no world and no goal, was a long way off. They would grub supply in the town and turn south toward San Antonio and the border.

"Anyhow," he mused aloud, "iff'n Little Moonlight don't git a saddle . . . or a hoss . . . she'll bump her bottom off on thet paint." He would wake Lone at high noon.

Josey didn't know the name of the town. They were here by chance, having struck the old Dallas–Waco road after midnight and turned off as the first streaks of light hit the east.

The town was Towash, one of many of the racing and gambling centers of central Texas. There was Bryan to the southeast, which gained fame of a sort when Big King, owner of the Blue Wing saloon, lost that establishment on the turn of a card to Ben Thompson, the Austin gambler and ex-Confederate pistol heller. Brenham, Texas, farther south of the

Brazos, was another center for the hard-eyed gentry of card and pistol.

Towash was a ripsnorter. The town is gone now, with only a few crumbling stone chimneys to mark its passing . . . west of Whitney. But in 1867 Towash made big sign . . . Texas-style. It boasted the Boles racetrack, which attracted the sports and gamblers from as far away as Hot Springs, Arkansas. There was a hand ferry across the Brazos and close by a grist mill powered by a huge waterwheel. Dyer & Jenkins was the trading store. There was a barbershop that did very little business and six saloons that did a lot, dispensing red-eye . . . raw. Typical of many towns in the Texas of 1867, there was no law except that made by each man with his own "craw sand." Occasionally the Regulators out of Austin rode in . . . always in large groups . . . more for protection than law enforcement.

When this occurred, it was the custom of the bartenders to move down the bar, rag-wiping as they went, announcing sotto voce, "Blue bellies in town." This for the benefit of all the "papered" gentry present. Some faded, and some didn't. In such cases another Texan often died with his boots on . . . but took with him a numbered thinning of the ranks of the Regulators in the fierce undeclared war of Reconstruction Texas.

A light whistle brought Lone to his feet. Little Moonlight squatted beside him as Josey talked and with a stick drew their future trail in the dirt.

"Ye goin' in too?" Lone asked.

Josey nodded, "We're way south, last they heard tell of me was the Nations."

Lone shook his head in doubt, "The talk is everywhere, and yer looks is knowed."

Josey stood up and stretched, "Lots of fellers' looks

is knowed. I ain't goin' to spend the rest o' my life wallerin' 'round in the brush. Anyhow, we ain't comin' back thisaway."

They saddled up in the late afternoon and rode down off the hillock toward Towash. Little Moonlight and the red-bone trailed behind.

12

Josey had not seen blue riders on the road because they were already in Towash. Led by "Lieutenant" Cann Tolly, twenty-four of them had quartered in two of the straggling log cabins that fronted the road on the edge of Towash. They were Regulators, and now they walked the street in groups of four and five, pushing their way with the arrogance of authority through the crowds and into the saloons. They were the same breed of men as their leader.

Cann Tolly had once tried to be a constable, wanting dominance over other men without the natural qualities that gave it to him. He had failed, miserably. When first called on to restore order in a saloon scuffle, he had been flooded with fear and had melted into a simpering, good-fellow attitude that brought laughter from the saloon toughs.

When the Civil War came, neither side held attraction for Cann Tolly. He affected a limp and as the War progressed he cadged drinks in saloons with tales of battles he had heard from others. He hated the returning Confederate veteran and the straight-backed Union cavalryman with equal ferocity. Most of all he hated the stubborn, tough Texans who had laughed at his cowardice.

Joining the Regulators gave him his badge of authority from the Governor, and he quickly toadied his way up in the ranks with the sadism that marks all men of fear . . . passing it off as "law" enforcement. Always backed by men and guns he tortured victims who showed fear in their eyes by insult and threat until the tortured men crawled lower than Cann Tolly crawled inside. Where he saw no fear he had them shot down with quick ferocity and so eliminated another "troublemaker." His was a false authority maintained by a false government. Lacking the true authority of respect by his fellow human beings, he enforced it with threat, terror, and brutality . . . and therefore . . . inevitably . . . must fall.

Lieutenant Tolly had spent the morning visiting those known peculiar dregs of the human race who take neither side of an issue but delight in ferreting out and betraying those who do. Clay Allison, the crippled pistoleer, had shot up Bryan three days ago and was believed headed this way. King Fisher had passed through town the day before, trailing back south . . . but had not stayed around for the fun . . . peculiar for a heller like Fisher, who loved games and action. But there would be enough to go around.

Late afternoon saw an end to the races, and the crowds poured back into Towash. The "boys," whoopin' it up, shot off their pistols and stampeded into the saloons to continue their betting urge at seven-up and five-card stud. The Regulators began looking them over.

It was into this confusion that Josey, Lone, and Little Moonlight rode their horses. Lone and Little Moonlight stayed mounted, as planned, across the street from the big sign that said "Dyer & Jenkins, Trade Goods." Josey rode to the hitch rack in front of the store, dismounted, and entered. To one side a crude bar stretched the length of the store, and jostling, laughing cowpunchers drank and talked. The trade-goods section was empty except for a clerk.

Josey called off his needs, and the clerk scurried to fill them. He would like to see the man gone as soon as possible. A man with two tied-down holsters was either a badman or a bluffer . . . and there weren't many bluffing men in Texas. Josey watched casually through the big window as blue uniforms sauntered down the boardwalks. Four of them paused across the street and looked curiously at the stoical Lone and then moved on. Two punchers circled the big black horse, admiring the fine points, and one of them said something to Little Moonlight. They laughed good-naturedly and walked into a saloon.

Josey selected a light saddle for the paint. He accepted the two sacks of supplies handed to him by the clerk and paid with double eagles. Now he moved slowly to the door and paused. Holding the saddle in one hand, he half dragged the two sacks with the other. With the easy air of a man checking the weather he looked up and down the boardwalk . . . there were no blue uniforms.

As he stepped to the walk he could see Lone start the black walking toward him . . . Little Moonlight behind . . . to take some of the supplies. He turned two

paces up the boardwalk toward his horse and came
face-to-face with Cann Tolly . . . and flanking him
were three Regulators. At the same instant he had
stepped from the store they had come out of the Iron
Man saloon. Fifteen paces separated them from Josey.

The Regulators froze in their tracks, and Josey, with
only the slightest hesitation, dipped his head and took
another step.

"Josey Wales!" Cann Tolly yelled the name to alarm
every Regulator in Towash. Josey dropped the saddle
and the sacks and fixed a look of bleakness on the man
who had shouted. The street became a clear distinct-
ness in his eyes. From the side he saw Lone halt his
horse. Men poured out of saloons and then fell back
against the sides of buildings. The boardwalk emptied,
and cowpunchers dived behind water troughs and
some flattened themselves on the ground.

He saw a young woman, her eyes a startling blue,
staring wild-eyed at him . . . her foot fixed on the hub
of a wagon wheel. She had been about to mount to the
seat, and an old woman held one of her hands. They
were both motionless, like wax figures. The girl's straw-
colored hair shone in the sun. The street was death-
quiet in an instant.

The Regulators looked back at him . . . half surprise,
half horror was on their faces. Another minute and the
Regulators all over town would recover from the mo-
mentary shock and he would be surrounded.

Josey Wales slowly eased into the crouch. His voice
shipped loud and flat in the silence . . . and it carried a
snarl of insult.

"Ye gonna pull them pistols, 'er whistle 'Dixie'?"

The Regulator to his left moved first, his hand darting downward; Cann Tolly followed. Only the right
hand of Josey moved. The big .44 belched as it cleared

leather in the fluid motion of rolled lightning. He fanned the hammer with his left palm.

The first man to draw flipped backward as the slug hit his chest. Cann Tolly spun sideways and made a little circle, like a dog chasing his tail, and fell, half his head blown off. The third was hit low, the big slug kicking him forward, and he flopped on his face. The fourth man was already dead from a smoking pistol held in the hand of Lone Watie.

It had been a deafening, staccato roar . . . so fast that a single shot could not be distinguished. The Regulators had never cleared leather. The awesome speed of the death-dealing outlaw ran through the crowd like tremors of an earthquake. Bedlam broke loose. Blue-clad figures ran across the street; people jumped and ran . . . this way and that . . . like chickens with a wolf among them.

Josey sprang to the back of the roan, and in an instant the big horse was running, belly-down, and at his saddle was the head of the black with Lone laying forward on his neck.

They drummed west down the street and veered north, away from the Brazos. They had to have distance, and there was no time to cross a river.

Regulators dashed for their hitch-racked horses, which stood, all together, before a line of saloons. As they were mounting, an Indian squaw, probably drunk, lost control of her paint horse and dashed among them, scattering men to right and left and stampeding horses that bolted, reins trailing, down the street. A Regulator finally struck her in the head with a swung rifle butt and brought her crashing to the ground. The riders mounted, rounded up the running horses, and chased after the fleeing killers.

Behind them Little Moonlight lay motionless in the

dust, a bloody gash across her forehead, but one hand still holding the reins of a head-down paint . . . a gaunt red-bone hound whined and licked the trickling blood from her face. Near her the four Regulators lay untended, sprawled in violent death, their blood widening in a growing circle . . . soaking black in the gray soil of Texas.

Cowboys mounted their horses to depart for the far-flung ranches whence they came. Gamblers left on their high-stepping horses to return to the saloons of towns and villages that were haunts. With them they carried the story. The story that smacked of legend. The pistoleer without match in speed and nerve . . . the cold bracing of four armed Regulators strained the imagination with its audacity and boldness. The Missouri guerrilla, Josey Wales, had arrived in Texas.

When the news reached Austin, the Governor added twenty-five hundred dollars to the federal five thousand for the death of Josey Wales, and fifteen hundred dollars for the unnamed "renegade" Rebel Indian who had notched a Regulator at Towash. Politicians felt the threat as the shock waves of the story spread over the state. The hard-rock Texas Rebels chortled with glee. Texas had another son; tough enough to stand . . . mean enough; enough to walk 'em down, by God!

Two covered wagons rolled out of Towash that afternoon and crossed the ferry on the Brazos, headed southwest into the sparsely settled land of the Comanche. Grandpa Samuel Turner handled the reins of the Arkansas mules on the lead wagon, and Grandma Sarah sat beside him. Behind them their granddaughter Laura Lee rode with Daniel Turner, Grandpa's brother. Two old men, an old woman, and a young one, with nothing left behind in Arkansas and only the promise of an isolated ranch bequeathed by Grand-ma's War-dead brother. They had been warned of the land and the Comanche . . . but they felt lucky . . . they had somewhere to go.

It was Laura Lee, Josey had seen, straw hair and prim, high-collared dress, frozen in the act of mounting the wagon. Now she shuddered as she remembered the burning black eyes of the outlaw . . . the deadly snarl of his voice . . . the pistols shooting fire and thunder . . . and the blood. Josey Wales! She would never forget the name nor the picture of him in her mind. Bloody, violent Texas! She would not scoff again at the stories. Laura Lee Turner would become a Texan . . . but only after baptism in the blood of yet another of Texas' turbulent frontiers . . . the land of the Comanche!

PART 3

PART 3

13

Josey and Lone let the big horses out. Running
with flared nostrils, they beat the dim trail into a thunder with their passing. One mile, two . . . three miles at
a killing pace for lesser mounts. Froth circled their
saddles when they pulled down into a slow canter.
They had headed north, but the Brazos curved sharply
back and forced them in a half-circle toward the northeast. There was no sound of pursuit.

"But they'll be comin'," Josey said grimly as they
pulled up in a thicket of cedar and oak. Dismounting,
they loosed the cinches of the saddles to blow the
horses as they walked them, back and forth, under the
shade. Josey ran his hands down the legs of the roan
. . . there wasn't a tremble. He saw Lone doing the same
with the black, and the Indian smiled, "Solid."

"They'll beat the brakes along the Brazos first," Josey said as he cut a chew of tobacco, "be looking fer a crossin' . . . cal'clate they'll be here in a hour." He rummaged in saddlebags, sliding caps on the nipples of the .44's and reloading charge and ball.

Lone followed his example. "Ain't got much loadin' to do," he said, "I was set to work on my end of the blues . . . but godamighty, I never seen sich greased pistol work. How'd ye know which one would go fer it first?" There was genuine awe and curiosity in Lone's voice.

Josey holstered his pistol and spat, "Well . . . the one third from my left had a flap holster and wa'ant of no itchin' hurry . . . one second from my left had scared eyes . . . knowed he couldn't make up his mind 'til somebody else done somethin'. The one on my left had the crazy eyes that would make him move when I said somethin'. I knowed where to start."

"How 'bout the one nearest me?" Lone asked curiously.

Josey grunted, "Never paid him no mind. I seen ye on the side."

Lone removed his hat and examined the gold tassels knotted on its band. "I could've missed," he said softly.

Josey turned and worked at cinching his saddle. The Indian knew . . . that for a death-splitting moment . . . Josey Wales had made a decision to place his life in Lone Watie's hands. He fussed with the leather . . . but he did not speak. The bond of brotherhood had grown close between him and the Cherokee. The words were not needed.

The sun set in a red haze behind the Brazos as Josey and Lone traveled east. They rode for an hour, walking the horses through stands of woods, cantering

them across open spaces, then turned south. It was
dark now, but a half-moon silvered the countryside.
Coming out of trees onto an open stretch, they nearly
bumped into a large body of horsemen emerging from
a line of cedars. The posse saw them immediately.
Men shouted, and a rifle cracked an echo. Josey whirled
the roan, and followed by Lone, pounded back toward the north. They rode hard for a mile, chancing
the uneven ground in the half-light and ripping
through trees and brush. Josey pulled up. The thrash-
ing behind them had faded, and in the far distance
men's shouts were dim and faraway.

"These hosses won't take us out of another'n," Josey
said grimly. "They got to have rest and graze . . .
they're white-eyed." He turned west, back toward the
Brazos. They stopped in the brakes of the river and
under the shadows of the trees rope-grazed the horses
with loose-cinched saddles.

"I could eat the south end of a northbound Missouri
mule," Lone said wistfully as they watched the horses
cropping grass.

Josey comfortably chewed at a wad of tobacco and
knocked a cicada from his grass-stem perch with a
stream of juice. "Proud I stuck this 'baccer in my pockets . . . leavin' all them supplies layin' in thet town.
And Little Moonlight's saddle . . ." Josey's voice trailed
off. Neither of them had mentioned the Indian
woman . . . nor did they know of her dash into the
horses that had delayed pursuit. Lone had anxiously
marked their progress north and had felt relief when
Josey had led back south. Little Moonlight would remember the trail, drawn with the stick on the ground,
southwest out of Towash. She would take that trail.

As if echoing his thought, Josey said quietly, "We
got to git south . . . somehow 'er 'nother . . . and

quick." Lone felt a sudden warmth for the scar-faced outlaw who sat beside him . . . and whose thoughts wandered away from his own safety in concern for an outcast Indian squaw.

They took turns dozing under the trees. Two hours before dawn they crossed the Brazos and an hour later holed up in a ravine so choked with brush, vine, and mesquite that the close air and late April sun made an oven of the hideout. They had picked the ravine for its rock-hard ground approach that would carry no tracks. Half a mile into the ravine, where it narrowed to no more than a slit cleaving the ground, they found a cavelike opening under thick vines. Lone, on foot, went back along their path and moved the brush and vines back into place where they had passed. He returned, triumphantly holding aloft a sage hen. They cleaned the hen, but set no fire, eating it raw.

"Never knowed raw chicken could taste so good," Josey said as he wiped his hands with a bunch of vines. Lone was cracking the bones with his teeth and sucking out the marrow.

"Ye oughta try the bones," Lone said, "ye have to eat ALL of ever'thing when ye're hungry . . . now, the Cheyenne . . . they eat the entrails too. If Little Moonlight was here . . . " Both of them left the sentence hanging . . . and their thoughts brought a drowsy, light sleep . . . while the horses pulled at the vines.

Near noon they were aroused by the beating of horses' hooves approaching from the east. The riders stopped for a moment on the lip of the ravine above them, and as Josey and Lone held their horses by the nose . . . they heard the riders gallop south.

Sunset brought the welcome coolness of a breeze that shook the brush and brought out the evening grouse. Josey and Lone emerged cautiously onto the prairie. No riders were in sight.

"East of us," Josey said, as they surveyed the land, "it's too heavy settled . . . we got to go west . . . then turn south."

They headed the horses westward toward a gradual elevation of the land that brought them, as they traveled, to a prairie more sparse of vegetation, where the elements were more rugged and wild.

In 1867, if you drew a line from the Red River south through the little town of Comanche . . . and keeping the line straight . . . on to the Rio Grande, west of that line you would find few men. Here and there an outpost settlement . . . a daring or foolhardy rancher attracted by that unexplainable urge to move where no one else dare go . . . and desperate men, running from a noose. For west of that line the Comanche was king.

Two hours after daylight Josey and Lone sighted the squat village of Comanche and turned southwest . . . across the line. They nooned on Redman Creek, a small, sluggish stream that wandered aimlessly in the brush, and at midafternoon resumed their journey. The heat was more intense, sapping at the strength of the horses as it bounced back off a soil grown more loose and sandy. Boulders of rock began to appear and stunted cactus poked spiny arms up from the plain. At dusk they rested the horses and ate a rabbit Lone shot from the saddle. This time they chanced a fire . . . small and smokeless, from the twigs of bone-dry 'chollo brush. Coarse grass was bunched in thick patches that the horses cropped with relish.

Josey had lived in the saddle for years, but he felt the weariness, sapped by lack of food, and he could see the age showing on Lone's face. But the rail-thin

Cherokee was eager for pushing on, and they saddled up in the dark and walked the horses steadily southwest.

It was after midnight when Lone pointed at a red dot in the distance. So far, it looked like a star for a moment. But it jumped and flickered.

"Big fire," Lone said, "could be Comanches havin' a party, somebody in trouble, or . . . some damn fool who wants to die."

After an hour of steady traveling, the fire was plainly visible, leaping high in the air and crackling the dried brush. It appeared to be a signal, but approaching closer, they could see no sign of life in the circle of light, and Josey felt the hairs on his neck rise at the eeriness. Still out of the light, they circled the flames, straining eyes in the half-light of the prairie. Josey saw a white spot that picked up the moonlight, and they rode cautiously toward it. It was the paint horse, picketed to a mesquite tree, munching grass.

Josey and Lone dismounted and examined the ground around the horse. Without warning, a crouched figure sprang from the concealment of brush and leaped on the half-bent figure of Lone. The Cherokee fell backward to the ground, his hat flying from his head. It was Little Moonlight. She was holding Lone's neck, astride him on the ground . . . giggling and laughing, rubbing her face on his, and snuggling her head, like a playful puppy, into his chest. Josey watched them rolling on the ground.

"Ye damn crazy squaw . . . I come near blowin' yer head off." But there was relief in his voice. Lone struggled to his feet and lifted her far off the ground . . . and kissed her fiercely on the mouth. They moved to the fire, where Josey and Lone extinguished it with

cupped hands of sand while Little Moonlight chattered around them like a child and once shyly clasped
the arm of Josey to her body and rubbed her head
against his shoulder. An ugly, deep gash ran the width
of her forehead, and Lone examined it with tender
fingers. "Ain't infected, but she could have shore stood
sewing up a day er two ago . . . too late now."

"By the time that'n scars over," Josey observed,
"she'll look like she stuck her haid in a wildcat's den . . .
ast her how she got it."

Little Moonlight told the story with her moving
hands, and as Lone repeated it to Josey, he listened,
head down. She laughed and giggled at the confused
Regulators, the running crowd, the stupefied people.
Her own actions, which caused the hilarious scene of
comedy, came out as an afterthought. She saw nothing
extraordinary in what she had done . . . it was a natural action, as proper as pot-cooking for her man.
When she had finished, Josey drew her to him and
held her for a long moment, and Little Moonlight was
silent . . . and moisture shone in the eyes of Lone
Watie.

"We'd better git away from where this house fire
was at," Josey said, and as they walked to the horses
Little Moonlight excitedly ran to a brush heap and drug
forth the new saddle that Josey had dropped in
Towash.

"Supplies, by God!" Josey shouted, "she got the supplies."

Lone gestured to her and made motions of eating.
"Eat," Lone urged. She ran and picked up a limp sack
and from it extracted three shriveled, raw potatoes.
"Eat?" Lone asked . . . and she shook her head. Lone
turned to Josey, "Three 'taters, looks like that's it."

Josey sighed, "Well . . . reckin we can eat the damn saddle after Little Moonlight tenders it up . . . bumpin' her bottom agin it."

Only after an hour's riding was Josey satisfied with their distance from the fire . . . and they bedded down. Noon of the following day they crossed the Colorado and lingered there in the shade of cottonwoods until sundown. Sun heat was becoming more intense, and it was in the cool of dusk before they saddled and continued southwest.

Their southwest direction would not take them to San Antonio, but Josey knew that after Towash they must avoid the settlements.

14

The Western outlaw usually faced high odds. Beyond their physical, practiced dexterity with the pistol and their courage, those who "done the thinkin'" were the ones who lasted longest. They always endeavored an "edge." Some, such as Hardin, stepped sideways, back and forth, in a pistol fight. They would draw their pistol in midsentence, catching their opponents napping. Most of them were masters of psychology and usually made good poker players. They concerned themselves with eye adjustment to light . . . or maneuvering to place the sun behind them. The audacious . . . the bold . . . the unexpected; the "edge," they called it.

To his reckless men Bloody Bill Anderson had been a master tutor of the "edge." Once he had told Josey,

"Iff'n I'm to face out and outlast another feller in the hot sun . . . all I want is a broom straw to hold over my head fer shade. A little edge, and I'll beat 'em." He had found his greatest student in the canny, mountain-bred Josey Wales, who had the same will to triumph as the wildcat of his native home.

So it was that Josey was concerned about the horses. They looked well enough, though lean. They ate the bunch grass and showed no lack of spirit. But too many times in the past years his survival had hung on the thread of his horse, and he knew that with two horses, given the same blood, breed, and bone, one would outlast the other in direct proportion to the amount of grain, rather than grass, that had been ra-tioned to it. The wind stamina made the difference, and so gave the edge to the outlaw who grained his horse . . . if only a few handfuls a day. The "edge" was an obsession with Josey Wales, and this obsession ex-tended to the horse.

When they crossed the wagon tracks in late after-noon of the following day Josey turned onto their trail. Lone examined the tracks, "Two wagons. Eight . . . maybe ten hours ago."

The tracks pointed west, off their course, but Lone was not surprised at Josey's leading them after the wagons. He had learned the outlaw's concerns and his ways, so that when Josey muttered an explanation, "We need grain . . . might be we could up-trade thet paint," Lone nodded without comment. They lifted the pace of the horses into a slow, rocking canter, and Little Moonlight alternately popped and creaked the new saddle as she bobbed behind them on the rugged little pony.

It was near midnight before Josey called a halt. They rolled in their blankets against the chill and were back in the saddles before the first red color touched the east. The elevation in the land was sharper since turning west, and by morning they were on the Great Plains of Texas. Where the wind had swept away loose soil, stark rock formations rose in brutal nakedness. Arroyos, choked with boulders, split the ground, and in the distance a bald mountain poked its barren back against the sky. As the sun rose higher, lizards scurried to the sparse shades of spiny cactus and a clutch of buzzards soared, high and circling, on their death-watch.

Heat rays began to lift off the baked ground, making the distant land ahead look liquid and unreal. Josey began to search for shade.

It was Lone who saw the horse tracks first. They angled from the southeast until they crossed the trail of the two wagons. Now they followed them.

Lone dismounted and walked down the trail, searching the ground. "Eight horses . . . unshod, probably Comanch," he called back to Josey. "But these big wide-wheel tracks . . . three sets of 'em . . . and they ain't wagons . . . they're two-wheel carts. I never heard of Comanches travelin' in two-wheel carts."

"I ain't never heard of anybody travelin' in two-wheel carts," Josey said laconically.

Little Moonlight had walked down the trail and now came back running. "Koh-mahn-chey-rohs!" she shouted, pointing at the track. "Koh-mahn-chey-rohs!"

"Comancheros!" Josey and Lone exclaimed together.

Little Moonlight moved her hands with such agitation that Lone motioned for her to go slower. When she had finished, Lone looked grimly up at Josey. "She says they steal . . . loot. They kill . . . murder the very old and the very young. They sell the women and strong men to the Comanche for the horses the Comanche takes in raids. They sell the fire stick . . . the gun to the Comanche. They have carts with wheels higher than a man. They sell the horses they get from the Comanches . . . like the two ye killed in the Nations. Some of 'em are Anglo . . . some Mexicano . . . some half-breed Indian."

Lone spread his hands and looked at the ground. "That's all she knows. She says she'll kill herself before she'll be taken . . . she says the Comanch will pay high price only for the unused woman and . . . her nose shows she has been used . . . that the Comanchero would . . . use her . . . rape her . . . many times before they sold her. That it would make no difference in her price." Lone's voice was hard.

Josey's jaws moved deliberately on a chew of tobacco. His eyes narrowed into black slits as he listened and watched the trail west. "Border trash," he spat, "knowed them two in the Nations was sich when I seen 'em. We'd best git along . . . them pore pilgrims in the waggins . . . "

Lone and Little Moonlight mounted, and in her passing, she touched the leg of Josey Wales; the touchstone of strength; the warrior with the magic guns.

The sun had slipped far to the west, picking up a red dust haze, when the tracks they were following suddenly cut to the left and dipped down behind a rise of rock outcroppings. Lone pointed silently at a thin trail of smoke that lifted, undisturbed, high into the air. They left the trail and walked the horses, slowly, toward the rocks. Dismounting, Josey motioned for Little Moonlight to stand and hold the horses while he and Lone stealthily walked, head down, to the top of the rise. As they neared the summit both bellied down and crawled hatless to the rim.

They weren't prepared for the scene a hundred yards below them. Three huge wooden carts were lined end to end in the arroyo. They were two-wheeled . . . solid wheels that rose high above the beds of the carts; and each was pulled by a yoke of oxen. Back of the carts were two covered wagons with mules standing in the traces. It was the scene twenty yards back of the wagons that brought low exclamations from Lone and Josey.

Two elderly men lay on their backs, arms and legs staked, spread-eagled on the ground. They were naked, and most of their withered bodies were smeared with dried blood. The smoke rising in the air came from fires built between their legs, at the crotch, and on their stomachs. The sick-sweet smell of burned human flesh was in the air. The old men were dead. A circle of men stood and squatted around the bodies on the ground. They wore sombreros, huge rounded hats that shaded their faces. Most of them were buckskin-trousered with the flaring chapparal leggings below the knees and fancy vests trimmed with silver conchos that picked up the sun with flashes of light. They all wore holstered pistols, and one man carried a rifle loosely in his hand.

As Josey and Lone watched, one of the men stepped from the circle, and sweeping the sombrero from his head, he revealed bright red hair and beard. He made an elaborate bow toward the corpse on the ground. The circle roared with laughter. Another kicked the bald head of a corpse while a slender, fancily dressed one jumped on the chest of a corpse and stomped his feet in imitation of a dance, to the accompaniment of loud hand-clapping.

"I make out eight of them animals," Josey gritted between clenched teeth.

Lone nodded. "There ought to be three more. There's eight hosses and three carts."

The Comancheros were leaving the mutilated figures on the ground and strolling with purpose toward the wagons. Josey looked ahead toward what drew their interest and for the first time saw the women in the shade of the last wagon.

An old woman was on her hands and knees, white hair loosened and streaming down about her face. She was vomiting on the ground. A younger woman supported her, holding her head and waist. She was kneeling, and long, straw-colored hair fell about her shoulders. Josey recognized her as the girl he had seen at Towash, the girl with the startling blue eyes, who had looked at him.

The Comancheros, a few feet from the women, broke into a rush that engulfed them. The girl was lifted off her feet as a Comanchero, his hand wrapped in her hair, twisted her head backward and down. The long dress was ripped from her body, and naked she was borne up and backward by the mob. Briefly, the large, firm mounds of her breasts arched in the air above the mob, pointing upward like white pyramids isolated above the melee until hands, brutally grabbing, pulled her down again. Several held her about the waist and were attempting to throw her to the ground. They howled and fought each other.

The old woman rose from her knees and flung herself at the mob and was knocked down. She came to her feet, swaying for an instant, then lowered her head like a tiny, frail bull and charged back into the mass, her fists flailing. The girl had not screamed, but she fought; her long, naked legs thrashed the air as she kicked.

Josey lifted a .44 and hesitated as he sought a clear

target. Lone touched his arm. "Wait," he said quietly
and pointed. A huge Mexican had emerged from the
front wagon. The sombrero pushed back from his head
revealed thick, iron-gray hair. He wore silver conchos
on his vest and down the sides of tight breeches.

"*Para!*" he shouted in a bull voice as he approached
the struggling mob. "Stop!" And drawing a pistol, he
fired into the air. The Comancheros immediately fell
away from the girl, and she stood, naked and head
down, her arms crossed over her breasts. The old
woman was on her knees. The big Mexican crashed his
pistol against the head of one man and sent him stag-
gering backward. He stomped his foot, and his voice
shook with rage as he pointed to the girl and turned to
point at the horses. "He is tellin' 'em they'll lose twenty
horses by rapin' the girl," Lone said, "and that they got
plenty of women at camp to the northwest."

A burst of laughter floated up from the Comancheros. "He jest told 'em the old woman is worth a . . .
donkey . . . and they can have her . . . if they think it's
worth it," Lone added grimly.

"By God!" Josey breathed. "By God, I didn't know
sich walked around on two legs."

The big leader drew a blanket from the wagon and
threw it at the girl. The old woman rose to her feet,
picked up the fallen blanket, and brought it around
the younger woman, covering her. Orders were shouted
back and forth; Comancheros leaped to the seats of
the carts and wagons. Another bound the wrists of the
two women with long rawhide rope and fastened the
ends to the tailgate of the last wagon.

"Gittin' ready to leave," Josey said. He looked at the
sun, almost on the rim of earth to the west. "They
must be in a hurry to make it to thet camp. They're
travelin' at night." He motioned Lone back from the

rimrock. Pulling Jamie's pistol and belt from his saddlebags, he tossed them to Lone. "Ye'll need a extry
pistol," he said and squatted on the ground before
Lone and Little Moonlight and marked with his finger
in the dust as he talked. "Put thet hat of yores on Little
Moonlight, thet Indian haid of yores will confuse 'em.
Ye circle on foot around behind. I'll give ye time . . .
then I'll hit 'em, mounted from the front. What I don't
git, I'll drive 'em into you. We got to get 'em ALL . . .
one gits away . . . he'll bring back Comanch."

Lone squashed the big hat down over the ears of
Little Moonlight, and she looked up, questions in her
eyes, from under the wide brim. "Reh-wan," Lone said
. . . revenge . . . and he drew a finger across his throat.
It was the cutthroat sign of the Sioux . . . to kill . . . not
for profit . . . not for horses . . . but for revenge . . . for a
principle; therefore, all the enemy must die.

Little Moonlight nodded vigorously, flopping the
big hat down over her eyes. She grinned and trotted
to the paint and slid the old rifle from a bundle.

"No . . . No," Lone held her arm and signed for her
to stay.

"Fer Gawd's sake," Josey sighed, "tell her to stay
here and hold the hosses . . . and keep thet red-bone
from chewing one of our laigs off." The hound had,
throughout, made low, rumbling noises in his throat.
Lone strapped the extra gunbelt around his waist.

"What if they don't run?" he asked casually.

"Them kind," Josey sneered, "always run . . . the
ones thet can. They'll run . . . straight back'ards . . .
they'll be trapped agin the walls of that there ditch."

Lone lifted his hand in half salute, and bent low,
moved silently on moccasined feet out of sight around
the rocks. Josey checked the caps and loads of his .44's
and the .36 Navy under his arm. Twelve loads in the

.44's . . . there were eight horsemen . . . three cart drivers . . . that made eleven; his mind clicked. He had counted only nine; the leader and the eight men. He whirled to stop Lone, but the Indian was gone.

Where were the other two men? The "edge" could be on the other side. Josey cursed his carelessness; the upsetting sight of the women . . . but there were no excuses . . . Josey bitterly condemned himself. Little Moonlight sat down, still holding the reins of the horses, with the rifle cradled in her arms. Josey slipped back to the rimrock and counted off the minutes. The sun slid below the mountain to the west, and a dusky red glow illumined the sky.

Mounted horsemen dashed up and down the line of carts and wagons. The canvas on one of the carts was being lashed down by a half-naked breed, and Josey looked for the women. They were standing behind the last wagon, close together, their hands tied in front of them. Josey slid back from the rim. It was time.

A shout, louder than the others, caused him to scramble up for a look. He saw two Comancheros dragging a limp figure between them. Other men on horses and foot were running toward the men and their burden, and for a moment obstructed his view. They pointed excitedly toward the rocks, and some of the mounted men rode in that direction, while others pulled their burden toward the rear of the last wagon where the two women stood.

They dropped their burden to the ground. The long, plaited hair . . . buckskin-garbed. It was Lone Watie. Josey cursed beneath his breath. The two missing Comancheros he should have figured. As he watched, Lone sat up and shook his head. He looked around him as the leader of the Comancheros approached. The big Mexican jerked the Indian to his feet and talked rapidly, then struck him in the face. Lone staggered back against the wagon and stood, staring stoically straight ahead. Josey watched them down the barrels of both .44's. Had a Comanchero raised a gun or knife . . . he would not have used it.

The big Mexican was obviously in a hurry. He shouted orders, and two men leaped forward, lashed Lone's hands together, and secured the rawhide to the tailgate of the wagon with the women. As they did . . . Lone raised his arms and wigwagged his hands back and forth. He did not look upward toward the rocks where he knew Josey watched. The hand signal was the well-known message of the Confederate Cavalry, "All well here, reconnoiter your flanks!" Josey read the message, and the shock hit him; *his flanks! . . . the Comanchero horsemen who had raced for cover behind the wagons!*

Josey scrambled down the rocks and ran toward the horses. He motioned Little Moonlight to mount, and leading the black, they raced toward the only immediate cover, two huge boulders that stood fifty yards from the arroyo. They had barely rounded the boulders when four horsemen appeared over the top. They paused and scanned the prairie but did not approach far enough to see the tracks. Turning, they ran their horses in the direction from which the wagons had come and then disappeared back into the arroyo.

A horrendous squealing rent the air, and the horses jumped. It was the carts moving . . . their heavy wooden wheels screeching against ungreased axles. Little Moonlight moved her horse next to Josey.

"Lone," she said. Josey crossed his wrists in the sign of the captive and then sought to reassure the fear that flashed in her eyes. His scarred face creased in a half grin. He tapped his chest and the big pistol butts in their holsters and moved his hands forward, palm down, in the sign that all would be well. Little Moonlight still wore the big hat of Lone's, and now she nodded, flopping it comically on her head. Her eyes lost the fear; the warrior with the magic guns would free Lone. He would kill the enemies. He would make things as they were.

Josey listened to the squealing carts growing fainter in the distance. It was dark now, but a three-quarter yellow Texas moon was just lifting behind broken crags to the east. A soft golden haze made shadows of the boulders, and a cooling breeze stirred the sagebrush. Somewhere, far off, a coyote yipped in quick barks and ended it with a long tenor howl.

Little Moonlight brought a thin handful of jerky beef from her bundle and held it out to Josey. He shook his head and motioned for her to eat. Instead, he cut a fresh cud of tobacco from the twist, hooked a leg over his saddle horn, and slowly chewed.

"Iff'n I don't git but half of 'em, they'll kill Lone and them women," he said half aloud. "Iff'n they make it to thet camp, they're shore gonna sport thet Cherokee with a knife and fire coals."

Josey was startled from his musing. The hound had lifted his voice in a deep, lonesome howl that ended forlornly in a breaking series of sobs. The red-bone jumped sideways, barely escaping the stream of tobacco juice.

"Ye damn Tennessee red-bone . . . we ain't huntin' 'possum 'er 'coon. Shet up!" The hound retreated behind Little Moonlight's paint, and she laughed. It was a soft and melodious laughter that made Josey look at her. She pointed to the moon . . . and at the dog.

"Let's go," Josey said gruffly, and he spurred the roan toward the arroyo.

15

Laura Lee Turner stumbled behind the wagon in the half-light of the moon. The high-button shoes were unsuitable for hiking, and she had already turned her ankles several times. The rough blanket tied around her shoulders irritated the burning skin where finger-nails had ripped away flesh on her back and stomach. Her breasts throbbed with excruciating pain, and her breath came short and hard. She had not spoken through her swollen lips since the attack . . . but that was not unusual for Laura Lee.

"Too quiet," Grandma Sarah had said when she came to live with her and Grandpa Samuel after her father and mother died of lung fever.

"Look, look, and whatta ye see, ain't right brite, Laura Lee," the children had sung around the log cabin schoolhouse, there in the Ozark Mountains . . .

when she was nine. She didn't go back to school. Kindly Grandma Sarah had shushed her when she'd say such things as, "Springtime's a'bornin' in this here thunderstorm," or "Clouds is like fluffy dreams a'floatin' crost a blue-sky mind."

Grandpa Samuel would look puzzled and remark, out of her hearing, "A leetle quare . . . but a good girl."

At fifteen, after taking her second box supper to a gathering in the settlement, she didn't go again. Grandpa Samuel had to buy hers . . . both times . . . in the embarrassment of the folks seeing one lone box left, and no boy would buy it.

"Ye'd ort to talk to 'em," Grandma Sarah would scold her. But she couldn't; while the other girls had chattered and giggled with the groups of boys, she had stood aside, dumb and stiff as a blackjack oak. She had large breasts, and her shoulders were square.

"Bones ain't delikit enough to attract these idjit whippersnappers," Grandma Sarah complained. The sturdy bones gave a ruggedness to her face that a preacher might charitably describe as "honest and open." The freckles across her nose didn't help any. Her waist was narrow enough, but she had a "heavy turn of ankle," and once when a backpack peddler had stopped by . . . and Grandpa had called her in for a shoe fitting, the peddler had laughed, "Got a fine pair of men's uppers will fit this here little lady." She had turned red and looked down at her twitching toes.

Grandma Sarah was practical, if disappointed . . . and resigned. She began preparing Laura Lee for the dismal destiny of unmarried maidenhood. Now, at twenty-two years of age, it was firmly settled; Laura Lee was an "old maid," and would so be, the rest of her life.

Grandma Sarah's bachelor brother Tom had sent the papers on his west Texas ranch, and when word reached them that he died at Shiloh, they made plans to leave the chert hill farm and take up the ranch. Laura Lee never questioned any thought of not going. There was nowhere else to go.

Now, stumbling behind the wagon, she had no doubt what awaited her. She accepted the fate without bitterness. She would fight . . . and then she would die. The wildness of this land called Texas had astonished her with its brutality. The picture of Towash flashed again in her mind; the picture of the scarred face, the searing black eyes of the killer, Josey Wales. He had looked deadly, spitting and snarling death . . . like the mountain lion she once saw . . . cornered against a rock face as men moved in upon it. She wondered if he were like these men into whose hands they had fallen.

Grandma Sarah stumbled along beside her. The long dress she wore cut her stride into short jerky steps, and sometimes she was forced to a half trot. Beside Grandma Sarah the captured savage walked easily. He was very tall and thin, but he strode with a lithe suppleness that denied the age of his wrinkled, oaken face, set in stoic calmness. He had said nothing. Even when the big Mexican had questioned and threatened him, he had remained silent . . . smiling, and then he had spat in the Mexican's face . . . and been struck backward.

She watched him now. Thirty yards behind them two horsemen rode, but she had seen the savage stealthily move the rawhide thong to his face twice before, and she was sure he chewed on it.

Dust boiled up in their faces from the squealing carts ahead, and a fit of coughing seized Grandma

Sarah. She stumbled and fell. Laura Lee moved to help her, but before she could reach the tiny figure the savage bent quickly and lifted her with surprising ease. He walked along, never breaking stride, as he held the little woman's tiny waist with his bound hands. He set her down and carefully kept his grip until Grandma Sarah had regained her stride. Grandma Sarah threw back her head to toss the long white hair back over her shoulders.

"Thank'ee," she mumbled.

"Ye're welcome," the savage said in a low, pleasant voice.

Laura Lee was stunned. The savage spoke English. She looked across at Lone, "You . . . that is . . . ye speak our language," she said haltingly, half afraid to address him.

"Yes, ma'am," he said, "reckin I take a swang at it."

Grandma Sarah, despite her jolting gait, was looking at him.

"But . . . " Laura Lee said, "ye're Indian . . . ain't ye?" She saw white teeth flash in the moonlight as the savage smiled.

"Yes, ma'am," he said, "full bred, I reckin . . . 'er so my pa told me. Don't reckon he had reason to lie about it."

Grandma Sarah couldn't contain any further silence. "Ye talk like . . . a . . . mountain . . . man," she jolted out the sentence from her half trot.

The Indian sounded surprised. "Why . . . reckin that's what I am, ma'am. Being Cherokee from the mountains of north Alabamer. Wound up in the Nations . . . leastwise, that is, 'til I wound up on the end of this here strang."

"Lord save us all," Grandma Sarah said grimly.

"Yes, ma'am," Lone answered, but Laura Lee noticed he had turned his head as he spoke and was scanning the prairie, as though he fully anticipated additional help besides the Lord's.

They lapsed into silence; the wagon was moving rapidly, and talking was difficult. The night wore on, and the moon passed its peak in the sky and dropped westward. It was cold, and Laura Lee could feel the chill as her naked legs opened the blanket with each stride. Once she felt the knot that held it loosening about her shoulders and she struggled futilely to hold it with her bound hands. She was surprised by the Indian suddenly walking close to her. He reached with his bound hands and silently retied the knot.

Grandma Sarah was stumbling more often now, and the Indian, each time, retrieved her and set her back in stride. He mumbled encouragement in her ear, "Won't be long, ma'am, before we stop." And once, when she seemed almost too weak to regain her legs, he had scolded her mildly, "Cain't quit, ma'am. They'll kill ye . . . ye cain't quit."

Grandma Sarah had a note of despair in her voice, "Pa's gone. 'Ceptin' Laura Lee, I'd be ready to go."

Laura Lee moved closer to the old woman and held her arm.

The moon hung palely suspended at the western rim when the streak of dawn crossed the big sky above them. Suddenly the wagon halted. Laura Lee could see a campfire kindled ahead and men gathering around it. Grandma Sarah sat down, and Laura Lee, sitting beside her, lifted her bound arms around the old woman and pulled her head down on her lap. She said nothing but clumsily stroked the wrinkled face and combed at the long white hair with her fingers.

Grandma Sarah opened her eyes. "Thank'ee, Laura Lee," she said weakly.

Lone stood beside them but he did not look toward the campfire ahead. Instead, he had his back to the wagon and gazed far off, along the way they had come. He stood like stone, transfixed in his concentration. After a long moment he was rewarded by catching the merest flicker of a shadow, perhaps an antelope . . . or a horse, as it dropped quickly over a roll in the plain. He watched more intently now and caught another shadow, moving more slowly, and curiously dotted with white, that followed the path of the first. His face cracked in a wolfish smile as he raised the rawhide to his teeth.

The sun rose higher . . . and hotter. The Comancheros were walking about now, stretching off the night's ride. The red-bearded man came around the wagon. Big Spanish spurs jingled as he walked. He carried a canteen in his hand and knelt beside Laura Lee and Grandma Sarah, and thrust the canteen into Laura Lee's hand.

"I'm gonna outbid the Comanch and breed you myself," he leered with a wide grin. Saliva and tobacco spittle ran down into his dirty beard. As he wiped his mouth on the back of one hand he slyly slid the other up her thigh. She struggled to rise, but he pressed himself down on her, one knee moving between her legs as he slipped a hand under the blanket and fondled her breasts. Lone plunged head down into the man with such force that he was knocked under the wagon. Laura Lee dropped the canteen. The Indian stood, implacable, as the red-bearded Comanchero cursed and thrashed his way to his feet. Without looking at Laura Lee, Lone said quietly, "Quick . . . the canteen . . . give water to Grandma . . . maybe her last chancet." She grabbed the canteen and tilted it to Grandma Sarah's lips as she heard the cracking thud of iron on bone, and the Indian fell beside her on the ground. He lay still, blood spurting over the coal-black hair.

Laura Lee was pouring water down Grandma Sarah. "Dadblame it, don't drown me, child," the old woman rose up, spluttering and choking.

The Comanchero grabbed the canteen, and Laura Lee fought him for it. She rose to her feet, twisting it from his grasp, and managed to splash water on the head of Lone. The Comanchero kicked her flat and retrieved the water. He was panting heavily. "You'll make a good lay when I bed you down," he spat. The scuffle had attracted more men toward the wagon . . . and he hurried away.

Laura Lee worked over the unconscious Lone. She turned him on his back and with the tail of her blanket clotted and stopped the blood flow. Grandma Sarah was up on her knees struggling with a string about her neck. She withdrew a small bag from the bosom of her dress. "Slap this asphitify bag under his nose," she instructed as she handed the bag to the girl.

Lone took one breath of the bag, twisted his head violently, and opened his eyes. "Beggin' yore pardon, ma'am," he said calmly, "but I never cottoned to rotted skunk."

Grandma Sarah's tone was weak but stern, "They'll shoot ye down iff'n ye cain't walk," she warned from her wobbly knees.

Lone rolled over on his stomach and brought himself to hands and knees. He stayed there a moment, swaying . . . then straightened up. "I'll walk," he

grinned through caked blood, "not much more walkin'
to do anyhow."

As he spoke, the wagon jerked, and Lone was forced
to hold Grandma Sarah up by the seat of her under-
wear to straighten her legs and get her in stride.

There was no pause at noon; the caravan rolled
steadily on, to the west. White alkali dust, mingled
with sweat, caked their faces into unreal masks, and
the sun heat sapped the strength from their legs. Now
Lone held a steady grip on Grandma Sarah; her trembling legs made half motions of walking, but it was
Lone who supported her weight.

The wagon began to drop downward as the caravan
moved into a deep canyon. It was narrow, with sheer
walls on either side, leveling off at the bottom. They
were headed, now, directly into the sun. Laura Lee
felt her legs trembling as she walked; she stumbled
and fell but scrambled to her feet without help. Suddenly the wagons halted. She looked across at Lone. "I
wonder why we've stopped?" Her voice sounded
cracked and coarse in her ears.

There was a triumphant smile on the Indian's face
. . . she thought he had become crazed from the blow on
his head. Finally, he answered her. "Iff'n I cal'clate
right, we're facin' directly into thet sun. These walls
hem us in. Thet would look like the thinkin' of a feller
I know what figgers all the edge he can git. I ain't
looked up ahead yet, but I'll bet my scalp a gent by
the name of Josey Wales has stopped this here train."

"Josey Wales?" Laura Lee croaked the name.

Grandma Sarah, from her knees on the ground,
whispered weakly, "Josey Wales? The killin' man we
seen at Towash? Lord save us."

Lone eased around the tailgate of the wagon. Laura

Lee stood beside him. Fifty yards ahead of them, astride the giant roan, standing squarely in the middle of the sun, sat Josey Wales. Lone shaded his eyes, and he could see the slow, meditative working of the jaws.

"Chawin' his tobaccer, by God," Lone said. He saw Josey look to the side with musing contemplation.

"Now spit," Lone breathed. Josey spat a stream of tobacco juice that expertly knocked a bloom from sagebrush. The Comancheros looked aghast, riveted into statues at this strange figure who appeared before them and evidenced such nonchalant interest . . . in aiming and spitting at sagebrush blooms.

Lone chewed vigorously at the rawhide on his wrists. "Git ready, little lady," he muttered to Laura Lee, "hell is fixin' to hit the breakfast."

The riders at the rear of the wagons came past and joined the others at the front of the caravan. Laura Lee shaded her eyes against the white light of the sun. "You speak of him . . . Josey Wales . . . as though he were your friend," she said to Lone.

"He is more than my friend," Lone said simply.

Grandma Sarah, still sitting, pulled herself around the wagon wheel and watched. "Even fer a mean 'un like him, they're too many of 'em," she whispered, but she held the wagon wheel and watched.

They saw Josey straighten in the saddle and slowly . . . slowly, he lifted a stick, at the end of which was attached a white flag. He waved it back and forth at the Comancheros, all grouped together at the head of the caravan.

"That's a surrender flag!" Laura Lee gasped.

Lone grinned through the mask of dusky face, "I don't know what he's figgerin' to do, but surrender ain't one of 'em."

The Comancheros were excited. There was agitated

talk, and argument developed among them. The big Mexican leader, mounted on a dappled gray, rode among the men and pointed with his hand. He selected the man with the red beard, another particularly vicious-appearing Anglo with human scalps sewed into his shirt, and a long-haired Mexican with two tied-down holsters.

The four horsemen advanced in a line, walking their horses cautiously toward Josey Wales. As they began their advance, Josey, as slowly, brought the roan to meet them. Silence, disturbed only by a faint moan of wind in the canyon rocks, fell over the scene. To Laura Lee the horses moved painfully slowly, stepping gingerly as their riders held them in check. It seemed to her that Josey Wales moved his horse only slightly faster . . . not enough to cause notice . . . but nevertheless, when they came together, facing each other, the roan was much closer to the wagons. They stopped.

She saw the scarred face of the outlaw plainly now. The same burning black eyes from beneath the hat brim. He rose slowly, standing in the stirrups as though stretching his body, but the subtle movement brought the angle of his pistols directly under his hands.

Suddenly the flag fell. She didn't see Josey Wales move his hands, but she saw smoke spurt from his hips. The BOOMS! of the heavy-throated .44's bounced into solid sound off the canyon walls. Two saddles emptied . . . the Mexican with tied-down holsters somersaulted backward off his horse. The red-bearded man twisted and fell, one foot caught in a stirrup. The scalp-shirted horseman doubled and slumped, and as the big Mexican leader half whirled his horse in a frantic rearing, a mighty force tore the side of his face off.

The speed and sound of the happening was like a

sharp thunderclap, causing a scene of mass confusion. The grulla horse of the red-bearded man came stampeding back upon the wagons, dragging the dead man by one foot. The half-crazed horse of the Mexican leader had been jerked, by his death grip, into a yoke of oxen. Out of the tangle, riding directly at them, Laura Lee saw the giant roan.

Josey Wales had two pistols in his hands. The reins of the roan were in his teeth, and as he crashed into the remaining horsemen bunched by the wagon, she saw him firing . . . and the earsplitting .44's bounced and ricocheted sound all around them. One man screamed as he fell headlong from his bucking horse; yells and cursings, frightened horses dashing this way and that. In the middle of it all, Laura Lee heard a sound that began low and rose in pitch and volume until it climaxed in a bloodcurdling crescendo of broken screams that brought pimples to her skin. The sound came from the throat of Josey Wales . . . the Rebel yell of exultation in battle and blood . . . and death. The sound of the scream was as primitive as the man. He swept so close by the wagon that Laura Lee shrank from the hooves of the terrible roan thundering down on her. Whirling the big red horse almost in midair, he brought him around behind a cart driver, half-naked . . . running on foot, and shot him squarely between the shoulders.

A Comanchero, his sombrero lying on his back, dashed by on a running horse and disappeared down the canyon. Josey whirled the big roan after him, and the hooves of their horses echoed down the canyon and diminished in the distance.

A fancily dressed Comanchero lying near Laura Lee raised his head. Blood covered his chest, and he looked across the open ground directly into her eyes. "Water

. . ." he said weakly, and tried to crawl, but his arms would not support the weight, "please . . . water." Laura Lee watched horrified as he tried again to pull himself toward her.

An Indian rose from the rocks of the canyon. Long plaited hair and fringed buckskin, but wearing a huge, flopping gray hat. The figure trotted up to the bloody Comanchero and stopped a few feet from him. As he lifted his hand . . . the Indian raised an old rifle and shot him cleanly through the head. It was Little Moonlight, with the scrawny red-bone shuffling at her heels. Now she dropped the rifle and advanced on them, pulling a wicked-looking knife from her belt. "Injuns!" Grandma Sarah shouted from her seat by the wagon wheel. "Lord save us."

Lone laughed. He, like the women, had watched the juggernaut of death that hit the camp with something akin to fascination . . . now the sight of Little Moonlight released the tension. She cut the thongs from his wrists, wrapped her arms around him, and laid her head on his chest.

A pistol shot in the distance rolled a rumbling echo up the canyon. Around them was the aftermath of the storm. Men lay in the grotesque postures of death. Horses stood head down. The grulla, coming from the head of the caravan, alternately walked and stopped, dragging the limp corpse by a stirrup. Except for the moan of the wind, it was the only sound in the canyon.

They saw Josey walking the horses. He was leading a sorrel that carried a pistol belt and sombrero dangling from the horn of an empty saddle. Behind the sorrel was Lone's big black.

The roan was lathered white, and froth whipped from his mouth. Josey pulled the horses to a halt in the shade of the wagon and politely touched the brim of his hat to Laura Lee and Grandma Sarah. Laura Lee nodded dumbly at his gesture. She felt awkward in the blanket and ill at ease. How did anybody act so calm and have company manners, like this man, after such violent death. A few minutes before he had shot . . . and yelled . . . and killed. She watched him shift sideways in the saddle and hook a leg around the horn. He made no motion to dismount as he meticulously cut tobacco with a long knife and thrust the wad into his mouth.

"Proud to struck up with ye agin, Cherokee," he drawled at Lone, "I would've rode on to Mexico, but I had to come and git ye, so ye could make thet crazy squaw behave."

Lone grinned up at him, "Knowed that'd bring ye."

"Now," Josey drawled laconically, "iff'n ye can git it 'crost to her, more'n likely these here two ladies would cotton to gittin' cut loose, a dab of water . . . clothes and sich as thet."

Lone looked embarrassed. "Sorry, ma'am," he mumbled to Laura Lee.

Little Moonlight got two canteens of water from the wagons, and as Laura Lee splashed cool water over her face, Lone knelt with a canteen for Grandma Sarah.

Josey frowned. "I was wonderin' about grain fer the hosses."

"I knowed ye'd ask that," Lone said dryly. "As I was ambling along behind this here wagon, whistlin' and singin' in the moonlight, I says to myself, I've got to take time from my enjoyment to check about the grain in these here wagons. I know Mr. Wales will likely come ridin' by d'rectly and lift his hat . . . and fust thing . . . ast about the grain."

Laura Lee was startled by the laughter of the two

men. Bloody corpses lay all about them. They had all
narrowly escaped death. Now they laughed uproariously . . . but instinctively, beneath the laughter, she
sensed the grim humor and a deep bond between the
Indian and the outlaw.

As though reading her thoughts Josey dismounted,
opened the flaps of the wagon, and taking her by the
arm, helped her into the back. "Set there, ma'am," he
said. "We'll scuffle ye some clothes." Turning to
Grandma Sarah, he lifted her in his arms and carefully
placed her beside Laura Lee. "There now, ma'am," he
said.

Grandma Sarah looked keenly at him. "Ye shore
bushwhacked all of 'em, looks like . . . them as was
fightin' and them as was runnin'."

"Yes, ma'am," Josey said politely. "Pa always said a
feller ought to take pride in his trade." He didn't ex-
plain that the "running" Comancheros would most
surely bring back Indians.

"My God!" Grandma Sarah screamed. Josey and
Lone whirled in the direction she pointed.

Little Moonlight, a knife in one hand and two
bloody scalps in the other, was kneeling beside the
head of a third corpse on the ground. Laura Lee pushed
farther back in the wagon.

"She don't mean nothin' . . . bad, that is," Lone said.
"Little Moonlight is Cheyenne. It's part of her religion.
Ye see, ma'am, Cheyennes believe there ain't but two
ways ye can keep from goin' to the Huntin' Grounds—
that is to be hung, where yore soul cain't git out of
yore mouth, and the other is being scalped. Little
Moonlight is makin' shore thet our enemies don't git
there . . . then we'll have it . . . well, more easy, when
we git there. Kinda like," Lone grinned, "a Arkansas

preacher sendin' his enemies to hell. Indian believes they ain't but two sins . . . bein' a coward . . . and turnin' agin yer own kind."

"Well," Grandma Sarah said doubtfully, "I reckin that's one way of lookin' at it."

Laura Lee looked at Josey, "Does she keep . . . the . . . scalps?"

Josey looked startled. "Why . . . I don't reckin, thet is, I never seen her totin' none around. But don't ye worry about Little Moonlight, ma'am . . . she's . . . kin."

Lone and Josey mounted their horses and with lariats dragged the bodies of the Comancheros far down the canyon into the boulders and rolled rocks over them. They had stripped them of guns and piled the guns and saddles they took from the horses into the wagons.

In his scouting Josey had discovered a narrow cleft in the far wall of the canyon, and near it a rock tank held clear water. He and Lone rummaged the three big carts and found barrels of grain, salt pork, jerky beef, dried beans, and flour. There were rifles and ammunition. All this they piled into the wagons; and with the eight horses tethered behind, Lone and Little Moonlight drove the wagons to the cleft in the canyon, as Laura Lee and Grandma Sarah rode with them.

The ground dropped down as it met the canyon wall, almost hiding the wagons from the trail. It was cool in the shadows, and they made camp at dusk; the high wall and cleft at their backs, the wagons before them.

Josey and Lone watered the horses and mules at the tank, and after picketing the mules near the wall on bunch grass and graining the horses, they led the six oxen to water. Laura Lee, in the wagon, heard Josey speaking to Lone, "We'll butcher one of the oxen in the mornin' and turn the rest of 'em loose. Might as well leave them carts where they are . . . they's all kind of stuff in 'em . . . old watches . . . picture frames . . . I seen a baby's crib . . . looted from ranches, I reckin."

She thought of the terrible Comancheros. How many lonely cabins had they burned? How many of the helpless had they tortured and murdered? The wretched, hoarse screams of Grandpa Samuel echoed in her ears, and the laughter of his tormentors. She sobbed, and her body shook. Grandma Sarah, beside her, squeezed her hand, and great tears rolled silently down her wrinkled face.

A hand touched her shoulder. It was Josey Wales. The yellow moon had risen over the canyon rim, shadowing his face as he looked up to her in the wagon. Only the white scar stood out in the moonlight. "Pick up yer clothes, ma'am," he said softly, "and I'll carry ye up to the tank . . . ye can wash. I'll come back and git Grandma Sarah."

He swung her in his arms, and she felt the strength of him. Timidly, she slipped her arm about his neck, and as he walked upward to the tank, she felt an overwhelming weakness. The horror of the past hours, the terror; now the overpowering comfort in the arms of this strange man she should fear . . . but did not. The blanket fell away, but it didn't matter.

He placed her on a broad, flat rock beside the pool of water and in a moment returned, carrying the frail Grandma Sarah. He knelt beside them. "I'll have to cut them shoes off ya'alls feet. Reckin ye'll have to wear boot moccasins, it's all we got."

As he slid the knife along the leather, Laura Lee asked, "Where is . . . the Indian?"

"Lone? Him and Little Moonlight is down there

brushin' out our tracks," he chuckled softly with secret humor, "they done washed in the tank."

Their feet were swollen, puffy lumps, and ugly cuts slashed by the rawhide swelled their arms. Josey stood up and looked down at them. "They's a little wall spring trickles water in this here tank . . . feeds out'n the other end. Stays fresh and cold . . . ought to take the swellin' down. Tank ain't but three foot deep. I'll be close by . . . " and he pointed, "up there, in the rocks."

He disappeared into the shadows and in a moment reappeared, silhouetted against the moon, looking past them into the canyon.

Laura Lee helped Grandma Sarah into the tank. The water was cold, washing over her body like a refreshing tonic.

"I couldn't help cryin'," Grandma Sarah said as she sat in the water. "I cain't help worryin' about Pa and Dan'l, layin' back there on the prairie."

The voice of Josey Wales floated softly down to them, "They was buried, ma'am . . . proper." Did his ears catch everything? Laura Lee wondered.

"Thank'ee, son," Grandma Sarah spoke as softly . . . and her voice broke, "God bless ye."

Laura Lee looked up at the figure on the rock. He was slowly chewing tobacco, looking out toward the canyon . . . and with a ragged cloth he was cleaning his pistols.

16

The morning broke red and hot and chased the chill from the canyon. Josey and Lone slaughtered an oxen and brought slabs of the meat to the smokeless fire Little Moonlight had built in a chimney crack of the canyon cleft. Laura Lee pushed a weakly protesting Grandma Sarah back on her blankets and walked to the fire on swollen feet.

"I can work," she announced flatly to Josey. Little Moonlight smiled and handed her a knife to slice the beef. Salting thin strips, they laid them on the flat rocks to cure in the sun, and it was late afternoon before they ate.

Laura Lee noticed that the two men never worked together. If one was working, the other watched the rim of the canyon. When she asked Josey why, he answered her shortly, "Comanche country, ma'am. This is their land . . . not our'n." And she saw that both he and Lone looked with studied concern at the spiral of circling buzzards that rose high in the air over the rocks that held the dead Comancheros.

They rested, filled with beef, in the dusk of shadows, against the canyon wall. Josey came to the blankets of Laura Lee and Grandma Sarah. He carried a small iron pot and knelt beside them.

"Taller and herbs Lone fixed. It'll take the swellin' down." He smoothed it on their feet and legs, and as Laura Lee blushed and timidly extended her leg, he looked up at her for a steady moment, "It don't matter none, ma'am. We do . . . what we have to do . . . to live. Ain't always purty . . . 'ner proper, I reckin. Necessary is what decides it."

Laura Lee lay back on the blankets and slept. She dreamed of a huge, charging red horse that bore down upon her, ridden by a terrible man with a scarred face who screamed and shot death from his guns. The deep howl of a wolf close by on the canyon rim awakened her. Grandma Sarah was sitting up, combing her hair. Close by in the shadows and facing her was Lone. Little Moonlight lay on the ground, her head on Lone's thigh. She didn't see Josey Wales. The soreness and swelling was gone from her feet.

"Is . . . where is Mr. Wales?" Laura Lee asked of Lone.

He looked toward the canyon valley flooded with the soft light of a nearly full moon. "He's here," he said softly, "somewhere in the rocks. He don't sleep much, reckin it's from years of brush ridin'."

Laura Lee hesitated, and her voice was timid, "I heard him say that he was kin to Little Moonlight . . . is he?"

Lone's laugh was low. "No, ma'am. Not like you mean. Where Josey come from . . . back in the mountains . . . the old folks meant different by thet word. If a feller told another'n thet he kin 'em . . . he meant he understands 'em. Iff'n he tells his woman that he kin 'er . . . which ain't often . . . he means he loves 'er." There was a moment of silence before Lone continued, "Ye see, ma'am, to the mountain man, it's the same thing . . . lovin' and understandin' . . . cain't have one without t'other'n. Little Moonlight here," and he laid his hand on her head, "Josey understands. Oh, he don't understand Cheyenne ways and sich . . . it's what's underneath, he understands . . . reckin loyalty and sich . . . and she understands them things . . . and well, they love thet in one 'nother. So ye see, they got a understandin' . . . a love fer one another . . . they're kin."

"You mean . . . ?" Laura Lee left the meaning in the question.

Lone chuckled, "No, I don't mean she's his woman . . . nothin' like thet. Reckin I cain't talk it like it is, ma'am . . . but Josey and Little Moonlight, either one would die flat in their track fer t'other'n."

"And you," Laura Lee said softly.

"And me," Lone said.

The night wind picked up a low sigh across the brush, and a coyote reminded them with his long howl of the distance and the loneliness of the desolate land. Laura Lee shivered, and Grandma Sarah placed a blanket around her shoulders. She had never asked questions . . . boldly of other people . . . but curiosity . . . and something more, overcame her reticence. "Why . . . I mean, how is it that he is . . . wanted?" she asked.

The silence was so long that she thought Lone

would not speak. Finally, his voice floated softly in the shadows, searching for words, "Iff'n I told ye that a lodge . . . a house was burnin' down, ye'd say thet was bad. Iff'n I told ye it was yore home thet was burnin' . . . and ye loved thet home, and them thet was in it, ye'd crawl . . . iff'n ye had to . . . to fight thet fire. Ye'd hate thet fire . . . but only jest as deep as ye loved thet home . . . not 'cause ye hate fire . . . but 'cause ye loved yer home. Deeper ye loved . . . deeper ye'd hate." The Indian's tone grew hard, "Bullies don't love, ma'am. They kill out'a fear and torture to watch men beg . . . tryin' to prove they's something low in men as they are. When they're faced with a fight . . . they cut and run. Thet's why Josey knowed he could whup them Comancheros. Josey is a great warrior. He loves deep . . . hates hard, ever'thing's that killed what he loves. All great warriors are sich men." Lone's voice softened, "It is so . . . and it will always be."

In the stillness Grandma Sarah felt for her hand and patted it. Laura Lee hadn't realized, but she was crying. She felt in Lone's words the loneliness of the outlaw; the bitterness of broken dreams and futile hopes; the ache of loved ones lost. She knew then what the heart of the implacable Indian squaw had always known, that true warriors are fierce . . . and tender . . . and lonely men.

It was early when she wakened. The sun was striking the top of the canyon rim, turning it red and moving its rays down the wall like a sundial. Little Moonlight was rolling blankets and packing gear into the wagons. Grandma Sarah, on her hands and knees over a big paper map spread on the ground, was pointing out to Josey and Lone, who squatted beside, different parts of the map. "It's in this valley, got a clear creek. See the mountains that's marked?" she was saying.

Josey looked at Lone, "What do ye say?"

Lone studied the map, "I say we're here," and he placed his finger on the map. "Here is the ranch she speaks of and the swayback mountain to its north."

"How fer?" Josey asked.

Lone shrugged, "Maybe sixty . . . maybe a hunnerd mile. I cain't tell. It's to the southwest . . . but we are goin' that way anyhow . . . to the border."

Josey was chewing on tobacco, and Laura Lee noticed his buckskins were clean and he was clean-shaven. He spat, "Reckin we'll take ya'll and the wag-gins, ma'am. Iff'n there's nobody there . . . we'll jest have to git ye up some riders . . . some'eres. Ye cain't stay, two womenfolk, by yerselves in this country."

"Look," Grandma Sarah said eagerly, "there's a town marked, called Eagle Pass . . . it's on this river . . . Rye-oh Grandee."

"That's Rio Grande, ma'am," Lone said, "and thet Eagle Pass is a long ways from yore ranch . . . this town here, Santo Rio, is closer . . . maybe some riders there."

As they talked, Laura Lee helped Little Moonlight load the wagons. She felt refreshed and strong, and the boot moccasins were soft on her feet. Little Moonlight was kneeling to gather utensils and smiled up at Laura Lee . . . the smile froze on her face, "Koh-manch," she said softly . . . then louder, so that Josey and Lone heard, "Koh-manch!"

Lone pushed Grandma Sarah roughly to the ground and fell on her. Josey took two swift strides and jerked Laura Lee backward as his body fell, full length, on hers. Little Moonlight was already stretched full length and head down.

The Comanche made no attempt to conceal himself. He was astride a white pony with the half-slump grace of the natural horseman. A rifle lay across his knees, and his black, plaited hair carried a single feather that waved in the wind. He was a half mile from them, silhouetted against the morning sun, but it was obvious that he saw and watched them.

Laura Lee felt the heavy breathing and the heartbeat of Josey. "He . . . has seen us," she whispered.

"I know," Josey said grimly, "but maybe he ain't been there long enough to count three women . . . and jest two men."

Suddenly the Comanche jerked his horse into a tight, two-footed spin and disappeared over the rim.

Lone ran for the mules and hitched them to the wagons. Josey pulled Laura Lee to her feet, "There's Comanchero clothes in the waggins . . . ye'll have to wear 'em . . . like menfolks," he said.

They put them on, big sombreros, flared chapparal pants. Laura Lee put on the largest shirt she could find; it was V'd at the neck, without buttons, and her large breasts seemed about to split the cloth. She blushed red . . . and still redder when she saw Little Moonlight changing clothes in the open.

"I reckin," Josey said hesitantly, "they'll have to do." There was a hint of awe in his voice. Grandma Sarah looked like a leprechaun under a toadstool, as the big sombrero flopped despairingly around her shoulders.

"Looks like a family of hawgs moved out'n the seat of these britches," she complained.

In spite of their predicament, Josey couldn't contain his laughter at the sight, and from a distance, Lone joined in, at the bunched, sagging trousers on the tiny figure.

"Sorry, ma'am," Josey said and burst into laughter again, "it's jest . . . thet ye're so little."

Grandma Sarah lifted the sombrero with both hands so she could better see her tormentors. "T'ain't the size of the dog in the fight, it's the size of the fight in the dog," she said fiercely.

"Reckin thet's right as rain, ma'am," Josey said soberly . . . and then, "Little Moonlight can drive one of the waggins," he said.

"I'll drive the other," Laura Lee heard herself saying . . . and Grandma Sarah looked at her sharply; she had never handled mules nor a wagon; and Grandma Sarah was torn between puzzle and pleasure at this growing boldness in what had been a shy Laura Lee.

17

They brought the wagons down from the walls of the canyon and moved up onto the plain, turning southwest across an endless horizon. Lone, on the black, led the way, far ahead. Little Moonlight and Grandma Sarah sat the seat of the lead wagon, and Laura Lee drove the second, alone. Behind her the Comanchero horses, stretched out in a long line, each roped to the horse ahead, were tethered to the tailgate of her wagon. Huge skin waterbags flopped at their sides like misplaced camel humps.

Lone set the pace at a fast walk, suitable for the big mules. Josey rode at the sides of the wagons and ranged the roan out and back, watching the horizon. He knew in a moment that Laura Lee had never handled mules. She had begun by sawing the reins and alternately slackening and tightening her pull . . . but she was fast to learn, and he said nothing . . . anyway, there was too determined a set to Laura Lee's jaw to talk about it.

Twice Josey saw small dust clouds over the rise of plain, but they moved out of sight. They night-camped in the purple haze of dusk, placing the wagons in a V and rope-picketing the mules and horses close by on the buffalo grass.

Lone shook his head grimly when Josey spoke of the dust clouds, "No way of tellin'. We know that Comanch ain't travelin' by hisself . . . and there's Apache hereabouts. Don't know which one I'd ruther tangle with . . . both of 'em mean'ern cooter's hell."

Josey took the first watch, walking quietly among the horses. Any band of wandering warriors would want the horses first . . . women second. The moon was bright, bringing out a coyote's high bark, and from a long way off, the lone call of a buffalo wolf. The moon had tipped toward the west when he shook Lone out of his blankets . . . and found Little Moonlight with him. Josey squatted beside them. "Proud to see ya'll set up homesteadin'," he said and was rewarded by Lone's grin and Little Moonlight kicking him on the shin.

As he stretched beneath the wagon bed Josey felt a comfort from the gnawing concern he had felt for the aging Cherokee and the Indian woman. Lone and Little Moonlight had found a home, even if it was just an Indian blanket. Maybe . . . they would find a place . . . and a life . . . on the ranch of Grandma Sarah. He would ride to Mexico, alone.

They broke camp before dawn, and when the first light touched the eastern rim they were ready to roll the wagons.

"Ya'll had better strap these on," Josey extended belts and pistols to the women. He helped Grandma Sarah tighten the belt around her little waist and held up the big pistol for her, "Ye'll have to use two hands, I reckin, ma'am . . . but remember, don't shoot 'til yore target is close in . . . and this here weapon's got six bites in it . . . jest thumb the hammer." As he turned to help Laura Lee she wrapped a hand around the handle of the big pistol and pulled it easily from the holster. "Why, them's natural-born hands for a forty-four," Josey said admiringly.

Laura Lee looked at her hands as though they were new additions to her arms. Maybe too outsized for teacups and parties. Maybe all of her was . . . but seems like she fit this place called Texas. It was a hard . . . even mean land . . . but it was spacious and honest with its savagery, unlike the places where cruelty hid itself in the hypocrisy of social graces. Now she placed a foot on the hub of the wagon and sprang to the seat; picking up the reins of the mules, she sang out, "Git up, ye lop-eared Arkansas razorbacks." And Grandma Sarah, leaning far out to further witness this sudden growth of a lust for life in Laura Lee, nearly fell beneath a wagon wheel.

Steadily southwest. The sun angling on their right, and heat shimmering the distance. They dry-camped that night on the slope of a mesa and pushed early at dawn, walking the mules at a fast pace.

On the fifth day after leaving the canyon, they crossed a straggling stream, half alkali, and after filling their bags, they moved on. "Water brings riders," Lone said grimly.

Imperceptibly, the land changed. The buffalo grass grew thinner. Here and there a tall spike of the yucca burst a cloud of white balls at its top. Creosote and catclaw bushes were dotted with the yellow petals of the prickly pear and the savagely beautiful scarlet bloom of the cactus. Every plant carried spike or thorn, needle or claw . . . necessary for life in a harsh land. Even the buttes that rose in the distance were swept clean of softening lines, and their rock-edged silhouettes looked like gigantic teeth exposed for battle.

It was on the afternoon of this day that the Indian riders appeared. Suddenly they were there, riding single file, paralleling the wagons boldly, less than a hundred yards away. Ten of them; they matched the stride of their horses to the wagons and looked straight ahead as they rode.

Lone brought his horse back at an easy walk and fell in beside Josey. They rode together for a distance in silence, and Josey knew Laura Lee had seen the Indians, but she looked straight ahead, clucking to the mules like a veteran muleskinner.

"Comanches," Lone said and watched Josey cut a chew of tobacco.

He chewed and spat, "Seen any more of 'em anywheres?"

"Nope," Lone said, "that's all there is. Ye'll notice they got three pack horses packing antelope. They ain't got paint . . . they're dog soldiers . . . that's what the Comanch and Cheyenne calls their hunters . . . them as has to supply the meat. They've done all right, and they ain't a raidin' party . . . but a Comanch might have a little fun anytime. These here hosses look good to 'em . . . but they're checkin' how much it'll cost to git 'em."

They rode on for a while without speaking. "Ye stay close to the waggins," Josey said, defiling a cactus bloom with a stream of juice. He turned his horse toward the Indians, and Lone saw four holstered .44's strapped to his saddle, Missouri-guerrilla style. He put the roan at an angle toward them, only slightly increasing the horse's gait.

During the next quarter mile he edged closer to the Comanches. At first the warriors appeared not to notice, but as he came closer, a rider occasionally turned his head to look at the heavily armed rider on the big horse who looked frankly back at him, apparently eager to do battle.

Suddenly the leader lifted his rifle in the air with one hand . . . gave an earsplitting whoop, and cut his horse away from Josey and the wagons in a run. The warriors followed. Raising loud cries and waving their rifles, they disappeared as quickly as they had come.

As he drifted his horse back by the wagons, Grandma Sarah lifted her umbrella sombrero with both hands in salute . . . and Laura Lee smiled . . . broader than he had ever seen.

Lone wiped the sweat from his forehead, "Thet head Comanch come mighty close when he lifted thet rifle."

"I reckin," Josey said. "Will they be back?"

"No . . ." Lone said, a little uncertainly, "they're packin' heavy . . . means they're a ways from the main body . . . and they ain't travelin' in our direction. Onliest reason they won't be . . . it jest ain't convenient fer 'em . . . but they's plenty of Comanche to go 'round."

It was late afternoon when they raised the swayback mountain, part of a ragged chain of jumbled ridges and buttes that stumbled across the land, leaving wide gaps of desert between them. Grandma Sarah stared ahead at them, and as they camped in the red haze of sunset, she watched the mountain for a long time. By noon the following day they could see the mountain clearly. It was, close up, actually two mountains that peaked at opposite ends and ran their ridges downward parallel to each other, giving the appearance, at a distance, of a single mountain sagged downward in its center. Lone headed the wagons for the end of the near ridge, as it petered out in the desert.

It was not quite sunset when they rounded the ridge and were brought up short at the panorama. A valley ran between the mountains, and sparkling in the rays of late sun, a shallow creek, crystal clear, ran winding down the middle and led away into the desert. They turned up the valley, a contrasting oasis in a desert. Gamma grass was knee high to the horses; cottonwoods and live oak lined the creek banks. Spring flowers dappled the grass and carried their colors all the way to the naked buttes of the mountains that loomed on either side.

Antelope grazing on the far side of the creek lifted their heads as they passed, and coveys of quail scattered from ground nests. The valley alternately widened and narrowed between the mountains; sometimes a mile wide, and again narrowing to a width of fifty yards, creating semicircular parks through which they passed.

Longhorn cattle, big and fat, grazed the deep grass, and Josey, after a couple of hours traveling, guessed there were a thousand . . . and later, more and more of the huge beasts made him give up his estimate. They were wild, dashing at the sight of the wagons into the narrow arroyos that split the mountains on each side.

Josey saw rock partridge, ruff and sharp-tail grouse along the willows of the creek, and a short black bear, eating in a green berry patch, grunted at them and trotted away into the creek, scattering a herd of magnificent black-tailed deer.

They moved slowly up the valley, the weary, sun-heated, dusty desert travelers luxuriating in the cool abundance. The sun set, torching the sky behind the mountain an ember red that faded into purple, like paints spilled and mixing colors.

The coolness of the valley washed in their faces; not the sharp, penetrating cold of the desert, but the close, moist coolness of trees and water that refreshed and satisfied a thirst of weariness. The moon poked a near-full face over the canyon and chased shadows under the willows along the creek and against the canyon walls. The night birds came out and chatter-fussed and held long, trilling notes that haunted on the night breeze down the valley.

Lone stopped the wagons, and the horses cropped at the tall grass. "Maybe," he said almost in hushed tones, "we ought to night-camp."

Grandma Sarah stood up in the wagon seat. She had laid aside the sombrero and her white hair shone silver.

"It's jest like Tom writ it was," she said softly, "the house will be up yonder," and she pointed farther up the valley, "where the mountains come together. Cain't . . . cain't we go on?" Lone and Josey looked at each other and nodded . . . they moved on.

The moon was two hours higher when they saw the house, low and long, almost invisible from its sameness of adobe color with the buttes rising behind it. It was nestled snugly in a grove of cottonwoods, and as they pulled up beside it, they could see a barn, a low bunk-house, and at the side, an adobe cook shack. Behind the barn there was a rail corral that backgated into what appeared to be a horse pasture circling back, enclosing a clear pool of water into which the creek waterfalled from a narrow arroyo. It was the end of the valley.

They inspected the house; the long, low-ceilinged front room with rawhide chairs and slate rock floor.

The kitchen had no stove, but a huge cooking fireplace with a Dutch oven set into its side. There was a rough comfort about the house; beds were made of timber poles, but stripped with springy rawhide, and long couches of the same material were swung low against the walls.

Unloading the wagons in the yard, in the shadows of the cottonwoods, Laura Lee impulsively squeezed the arm of Josey and whispered, "It's like a . . . a dream."

"It is that," Josey said solemnly . . . and he wondered how Tom Turner must have felt, stumbling across this mere slit of verdant growth in the middle of a thousand square miles of semiarid land. He judged the valley to be ten . . . maybe twelve miles long. With natural grass, water, and the hemming walls of the mountains, two, maybe three riders could handle it all, except for branding and trailing time, when extras could be picked up.

He was jarred from his reverie when he saw Lone and Little Moonlight walking close together toward the little house that set back in a grove of red cedars and cottonwood. The place had got hold of him . . . hell, fer a minute he was figurin' like it was home.

Laura Lee and Grandma Sarah were fidgeting about in the house. Nobody would sleep this night. He unhitched the mules and led them with the horses to the corral and pasture. Leaning on the rail of the corral, he watched them circle, kick their heels, and head for the water of the clear pool. The big mules rolled in the high grass. He brought the big roan last, unsaddled him, and lovingly rubbed him down. He turned him loose with the others . . . but first he fed him grain.

Laura Lee whipped up biscuits for their breakfast

and fried the jerky beef with beans in the tallow of the oxen. The women busied themselves flying dust and dirt out the windows and doors and bustling with all the mysterious doin's women do in new houses. Little Moonlight had clearly laid claim to the adobe in the cedars and appropriated blankets, pots, and pans, which she industriously trotted from the pile of belongings in the backyard. Lone and Josey carried water from the waterfall and filled the cedar water bins in the house. They patched the corral fences and cleaned the guns, stacking and hanging them in the rooms, in easy reach. Lone set traps on the creek bank, and they suppered on golden bass.

After supper Josey and Lone squatted in the shadows of the trees and watched the moon rise over the canyon rim. The murmur of talk drifted to them from the kitchen where Laura Lee and Grandma Sarah washed up the supper plates, and through the window the flicker of firelight took the edge off a light spring chill. Little Moonlight sat before the door of the 'dobe in the cedars and faintly hummed in an alto voice the haunting, wandering melody of the Cheyenne.

"It is her lodge," Lone said. "She's told me it's the first time she has a lodge of her own."

"Reckin it's her'n and yore'n," Josey said quietly.

Lone shifted uncomfortably, "The woman . . . I never thought, old as I am . . . this place is like when I was a boy . . . a young man . . . back there. . . . " His voice trailed off in a helpless apology.

"I know," Josey said. He knew what the Indian could not say. Back there, back beyond the Trail of Tears . . . back there in the mountains there had been such a place; the home . . . the woman. And now it was given to him again; but he fretted against what he felt was somehow . . . disloyalty to the outlaw. Josey spoke, and his voice was matter-of-fact and held no emotion, "Ye ain't knowed . . . by name. We'll git the riders, but I couldn't leave Laura Lee . . . the women-folks, without I knowed they was somebody to be trusted . . . to boss and look after. Ye must stay here . . . ye and Little Moonlight . . . she's near good as a man . . . better'n most. Ain't no other way. Besides, I'll be trailin' back this way and more'n likely need a place to hole up."

Lone touched the shoulder of Josey, "Maybe," he said, "maybe they'll fergit about ye, and . . ."

Josey cut a chew of tobacco and studied the valley below them. There was no use saying it . . . they both knew there would be no forgetting.

18

Ten Bears trailed north from wintering in the land of the Mexicano, below the mysterious river that the pony soldiers refused to cross. Behind him rode five subchiefs, 250 battle-hardened warriors and over 400 squaws and children. Glutted with loot and scalps from raids on the villages and ranchos to the south, they had come back over the Rio Grande two days ago. They came back, as they had always done in the spring . . . as they always would do. The ways of the Comanche would not be shackled by the pony soldier, for the Comanche was the greatest horseman of the Plains and each of his warriors was equal to 100 of the bluecoats.

Ten Bears was the greatest of the war chiefs of the mighty Comanche. Even the great Red Cloud of the

Oglala Sioux, far to the north, called him a Brother Chief. There was no rivalry in all his subchiefs, for his place, his fame, was legend. He had led his warriors in hundreds of raids and battles and had tested his wisdom and courage a thousand times without blemish. He was eloquent in the speech of the white man, and last fall, as the buffalo grass turned brown, he had met General Sherman on the Llano Estacado and had told him the ways of the Comanche would not change. Ten Bears always kept his word.

When he had received the message that the bluecoat General wished to meet with him, he had at first refused. There had been four meetings in five years, and each time the white man offered his hand in friendship, while with the other hand he held the snake. At each meeting there was a new face of the bluecoat, but the words were always the same.

Finally he had agreed and selected the Llano Estacado as the meeting site . . . for this was the Staked Plain that the white man feared to cross; where the Comanche rode with impunity. It was a fit setting in the eyes of Ten Bears.

He had refused to sit, and while the bluecoat leader talked, he had stood, arms folded in stony silence. It was as he had suspected; much talk of friendship and goodwill for the Comanche . . . and orders for the Comanche to move farther toward the rim of the plain, where the sun died each day.

When the bluecoat had finished, Ten Bears had spoken in a voice choked with anger, "We have met many times before, and each time I have taken your hand, but when your shadow grew short upon the ground, the promises were broken like dried sticks beneath your heel. Your words change with the wind and die without meaning in the desert of your breast.

If we had not given up the lands you now hold, then we would have something to give for more of your crooked words. I know every water hole, every bush and antelope, from the land of the Mexicano to the land of the Sioux. I ride, free like the wind, and now I shall ride even until the breath that blows across this land breathes my dust into it. I shall meet you again only in battle, for there is iron in my heart."

He had stalked away from the meeting, and he and his warriors had burned and looted the ranches as they rode south through Texas into Mexico. Now he was returning, and hatred smoldered in his eyes . . . and in the eyes of the proud warriors who rode with him.

It was late on a Sunday afternoon when Ten Bears rounded the ridge of the mountains to make medicine in the cool valley . . . and saw the tracks of the wagons.

That same Sunday morning, the gathering for services took place in the shade of the cottonwoods that surrounded the ranch house. Grandma Sarah had announced it firmly at breakfast, "It's a Sunday, and we'all will observe the Lord's day."

Josey and Lone stood, awkwardly bareheaded; Little Moonlight between them. Laura Lee, still moccasined, but wearing a snow-white dress that accentuated the fullness of her figure, opened the Bible and read. It was a slow process. She moved her finger from word to word and bent her sun-browned face studiously over the pages: "Yea, though I walk through the valley of the shadow of death, I will fear no evil, for Thou art with me. Thy rod and Thy staff, they comfort me. . . ."

It took a long time, and Little Moonlight watched a house wren building a nest in a crack of the 'dobe.

With a great sigh of triumph, Laura Lee finished the Psalm, and Grandma Sarah looked sternly at her little congregation, expending a particularly lingering look at Little Moonlight. "Now we'll pray," she said, "and ever'body's got to hold hands."

Lone grasped the hand of Grandma Sarah and Little Moonlight; Josey took the right hand of Little Moonlight and extended his right to hold the hand of Laura Lee. He felt her tremble . . . and he thought he felt a squeeze. Little Moonlight perked up . . . there was more to the white man's ceremony.

"Bow yore heads," Grandma Sarah said, and Lone pushed Little Moonlight's head down.

"Lord," Grandma Sarah began in stentorian tones, "we're right sorry we ain't had time to observe and sich, but Ye've seen like it is. We ast Ye to look after Pa and Dan'l, they was . . . 'ceptin' a little liquorin' up, occasional . . . good men, better'n most, and they fit best they could agin that low-down, murderin' trash out o' hell that done 'em in. They died tol'able well, considerin', and," her voice broke, and she paused for a moment, ". . . and we thankee Ye seen fit to send one to bury 'em proper. We thankee fer this here place and ast Ye bless Tom's bones at Shiloh. We don't ast much, Lord . . . like them horned toads back East, wallerin' around in fine fittin's and the sin of Sodom. We be Texans now, fit'n to stand on our feet and fight fer what's our'n . . . with occasional help from Ye . . . Ye be willin'. We thankee fer these men . . . fer the Indian woman . . . " here, Grandma Sarah opened one eye and looked cannily at the bowed head of Josey Wales, ". . . and we thankee fer a good, strong, maidenly girl sich as Laura Lee . . . fit to raise strappin' sons and daughters to people this here land . . . iff'n she's give half a chancet. We thankee fer Josey Wales deliverin' us from the Philistines. Amen."

Grandma Sarah raised her head and sternly scanned

the circle. "Now," she said, "we'll end the service, ren-
derin' the song 'Sweet Bye and Bye.' " Lone and Josey
knew the song, and hesitantly at first, then joining
their voices with Laura Lee and Grandma Sarah, they
sang:

> "In the sweet bye and bye,
>   we shall meet on that beautiful shore,
> In the sweet bye and bye,
>   we shall meet on that beautiful shore."

They sang the chorus . . . and stumbled a bit over
the verses. Little Moonlight enjoyed this part of the
white man's ceremony most. She began a slow shuffle
of her feet that picked up tempo as she danced around
the circle; and though she didn't know the words, she
brought a peculiarly appealing harmony to it with an
alto moan. The red-bone flopped on his haunches and
began a gathering howl that added to the scene, growing in noise if not melody. Josey reached back a booted
toe to delicately, but viciously, kick him in the ribs.
The hound snarled.

It was . . . all in all . . . a satisfying morning, as
Grandma Sarah opined over a bounteous Sunday dinner; something they could all look forward to, each
and ev'ry Sunday morning.

19

The scouts told him that only two of the horses were ridden, and Ten Bears knew the meaning of the wagons . . . white squaws. He ordered the camp set boldly in the open at the foot of the valley. Ten Bears took pride in the order of the tight, tidy circles of tepees that marked the strict, disciplined ways of the Comanche. They were not slovenly as had been the Tonkaways, and the Tonkaways lived no more; the Comanche had killed them all.

Ten Bears had hated and despised the Tonkaways. It had been rumored throughout the Comanche Nation, as well as the Kiowa and Apache, that the Tonkaways were human flesh eaters. Ten Bears knew that they were. As a young warrior, having just passed his test of manhood and inexperienced in the ways of the trail, he had been captured by them; he and Spotted Horse, another youthful brave.

They had been bound, and that night, as the Tonkaways sat around their fire, one of them rose and came to them. He had a long knife in his hand, and he had sliced a piece of flesh from Spotted Horse's thigh and carried it back and roasted it over the flames. Others had come with their knives and sliced the flesh from Spotted Horse; his legs and his groin, and in the friendliest manner had complimented him over the taste of his own flesh.

When they had hit the fountains of blood, they had brought firebrands to stop the flow . . . so to keep Spotted Horse alive longer. Ten Bears and Spotted Horse had cursed them . . . but Spotted Horse had not cried out in fear or pain, and as he grew weaker, he began his death song.

When the Tonkaways slept, Ten Bears had slipped his bonds, but instead of running he had used their own weapons to kill them. With the captured horses bearing the stripped skeleton of Spotted Horse and a dozen scalps, he had ridden, splattered with the blood of his enemies, back to the Comanche. He had not washed the blood from his body for a week, and the story chant of Spotted Horse and the courage of Ten Bears was sung in all the lodges of the Comanche. It had been the beginning of Ten Bears' rise to power and the beginning of the end for the Tonkaways.

Now, in the gathering dusk of evening, the sub-chiefs had their squaws set their separate fires along the cool creek. Their tepees blocked any entrance . . . or escape . . . from the valley.

Ten Bears knew of the white man's lodge at the end of the valley, where the canyon walls came together. He had settled there during the period of peace, after a meeting of Comanche and bluecoat, and more promises that would be broken. Ten Bears once had come to kill him and to kill his Mexicano riders . . . but when he and his warriors had ridden to the house, they had found no one.

Everything was still in order in the white man's lodge; the hard leaves from which the white man ate were set on his ceremonial table; the food was in the lodge, as were his blankets. True, the horses of the man and his Mexicano riders were gone, but the Comanches knew that no man would leave without his blankets and his food . . . and so they knew as certainly that the man and his riders had been snatched from the earth because of Ten Bears' displeasure. They had not disturbed the white man's lodge . . . it would be bad medicine.

Later, in the settlements, Ten Bears had learned that the man had gone to join the Gray Riders, who were fighting the bluecoats . . . but he had not told his warriors; they would have listened and accepted his words . . . but they had seen with their own eyes the evidence of mysterious disappearance. Besides . . . it added to the stature of Ten Bears' legend. Let them believe as they wished.

Ten Bears stood alone before his tepees as his women made food. He looked contemptuously at the medicine men as they began their chant. He had stopped the medicine dances when he found that the medicine men were accepting bribes of horses from braves who did not want to dance in the exhausting routine, the test of stamina that would decide if medicine was good or bad. Like religious leaders everywhere, they sought power and wealth, and so had become double-tongues, like the politicians. Ten Bears looked on them with the inborn disgust of the warrior.

He allowed them their chants and their prattlings of omen and signs, pomp, and ceremony . . . but he paid no attention to their advice nor their superstitions.

Now, with a few words and a wave of his arm, he sent riders along the rim of the canyon to station themselves and watch the lodge of the white men. There would be no escape in the morning.

Josey slept lightly in his bedroom across the hall from Laura Lee. He had not yet accustomed himself to the walls and roof . . . nor the silence away from the night sounds of the trails. Each night Laura Lee had heard him rise several times and walk softly down the stone-floored hall and then return.

She knew it was late when the low whistle wakened her. It had come from the thin, rifle-slot window of Josey's room, and she heard his walk, quick and soft, down the hall. She followed him on bare feet, a blanket wrapped around her nightgown, and stood in the shadows, out of the square of moon that shone on the kitchen floor. It was Lone who met Josey on the back porch . . . and she heard them talk.

"Comanches," Lone said, "all around us on the rims." His clothes were wet, and water dripped into little puddles on the rough boards.

"Where ye been?" Josey asked quietly.

"Down the creek, all the way. There's an army of 'em down there . . . maybe two, three hunnerd warriors . . . lot of squaws. It ain't no little war party. They're makin' medicine . . . so I stayed in the creek and got close to read sign. And listen to this . . ." Lone paused to give emphasis to his news . . . "ye know the sign on the Chief's tepee? . . . It's Ten Bears! Ten Bears, by God! The meanest hunk o' walkin' mad south of Red Cloud."

Laura Lee shivered in the darkness. She heard Josey ask,

"Why ain't they done hit us?"

"Well," Lone said, "thet moon is a Comanche moon all right . . . meanin' it's plenty light enough to raid . . . with plenty light fer the Happy Huntin' grounds if one of 'em died . . . but they're makin' medicine fer big things, probably ridin' north. They'll hit us in the mornin' . . . and that'll be it. There's too many of 'em."

There was a long pause before Josey asked, "Any way out?"

"No way . . ." Lone said, "sayin' we could slip by them that's on the rim . . . we'd have to go afoot up them walls, and they'd track us down in the mornin', out in the open, with no horses."

Again, a long period of silence. Laura Lee thought they had walked away and was about to peer around the door when she heard Josey.

"No way," he said.

"Git Little Moonlight," Josey ordered harshly and came back into the kitchen. He bumped full into Laura Lee standing there, and she impulsively threw her arms around his neck.

Slowly he embraced her, feeling the eagerness of her body against him. She trembled, and easily, naturally, their lips came together. Lone and Little Moonlight found them this way when they returned, standing in soft beams of the moon that filtered through the kitchen door. Josey's hat had fallen to the floor, and it was Little Moonlight who retrieved it and handed it to him.

"Git Grandma," he said to Laura Lee.

In the half-light of the kitchen Josey spoke in the cold, flat tone of the guerrilla chieftain. The blood drained from Grandma Sarah's face as their situation became clear, but she was tight-lipped and silent. Little Moonlight, holding a rifle in one hand, a knife in the other, stood by the kitchen door, looking toward the canyon rim.

"Iff'n I was lookin' fer a place fer a hole-up fight," he said, "I'd pick this 'un. Walls and roof is over two foot thick, all mud, and nothin' to burn. Jest two doors, front and back, and in sight of each other. These narrer crosses we call winders is fer rifle fire . . . up and down . . . and side to side, and cain't nobody come through 'em. The feller . . . Tom . . . thet built the house, ye'll notice, put these crossed winders all around, no blind spots; we got 'em right by each door. Little Moonlight will fire through that'n . . ." he pointed toward the heavy door that opened into the front of the house, "and Laura Lee will fire through this'n, by the back door."

Josey took a long step to stand in the wide space of floor that separated the kitchen from the living room. "Grandma will set here," he said, "with the buckets of powder, ball, and caps, and do the loadin' . . . can ye handle thet, Grandma?"

"I kin handle it," Grandma Sarah said tersely.

"Now Lone," Josey continued, "he'll fill in firing where at the rush is, and on towards the end, he'll be facin' thet hallway runs down by the bedrooms and keepin' fire directed thataway."

"Why?" Laura Lee asked quickly, "why would Lone be firing down the hall?"

" 'Cause," Josey said, "onliest blind spot is the roof. They'll finally git around to it. We cain't fire through the roof. Too thick. They'll dig a dozen holes to drop through back there in the bedrooms. That's why we're goin' to stack logs here at the door to the hall. All we're defendin' is these here two doors and space 'twixt 'em. When we git to thet part," he added grimly, "the fight will be 'bout over, one way or t'other'n. It'll be a last drive they'll make. Remember this . . . when things git plumb wuss . . . where it's liken to be ye cain't make it . . . thet means it's all goin' to be decided right quick . . . cain't last long. Then ye got to git mean . . . dirty mean . . . ye got to git plumb mad-dog mean . . . like a heller . . . and ye'll come through. Iff'n ye lose yore head and give up . . . ye're finished and ye ain't deservin' of winnin' ner livin'. Thet's the way it is."

Now he turned to Lone, who was leaning against the kitchen wall. "Use pistols short range . . . less reloadin', more firepower. We'll start a fire 'bout dawn in the fireplace and put iron on it . . . keep the iron red hot. Anybody gits hit . . . sing out . . . Lone'll slap the iron to it . . . ain't got time to stop blood no other way."

Josey looked at their faces. Tense, strained . . . but not a tear nor a whimper in the whole lot. Solid stuff, clear to the marrow.

They worked in the dark, bringing water to fill the bins and piling the pistols and rifles of the Comancheros on the kitchen table. There were twenty-two Colts' .44's and fourteen rifles. Lone checked the loads of the guns. They placed the kegs of powder, ball, and caps in the middle of the floor and stacked heavy logs, head high, with only room for a pistol barrel between them, at the door to the hall.

It was still dark when they rested . . . but the early morning twittering of birds had already begun. Grandma Sarah brought out cold biscuits and beef, and they ate in silence. When they had finished, Josey pulled off his buckskin jacket. The butternut-colored guerrilla shirt was loose fitting, almost like a woman's blouse. The .36 Navy Colt protruded from beneath his left shoulder.

He handed the jacket to Laura Lee, "Reckin I won't be needin' this," he said, " 'preciate it, iff'n ye'll keep it fer me." She took the jacket and nodded dumbly. Josey had turned to Lone and drawled, "Reckin I'll be saddlin' up now."

Lone nodded, and Josey was through the door and walking to the corral before Laura Lee and Grandma Sarah recovered the sense of what he had said.

"What . . . ?" Grandma Sarah said, startled. "Whar's he a-goin'?"

Laura Lee raced for the door, but Lone grabbed her by the shoulders and held her in a firm grip.

"Woman talk is no good fer him now," Lone said.

"Where's he goin' . . . what's happening?" she said frantically.

Lone pushed her back from the door and faced the women. "He knows he can do the best fer us on the back of a hoss. He's a guerrilla . . . they always figger to carry the fight to the enemy, and now he goes to do so again." Lone spoke slowly and carefully, "He is goin' into the valley to kill Ten Bears and many of his chiefs and warriors. When the Comanche comes to us . . . the head of the Comanche will be crushed . . . and his back broken. Josey Wales will do this, so thet . . . if we do as he has said we should do . . . we will live."

"Lord God Almighty!" Grandma Sarah said in hushed tones.

Laura Lee whispered, "He is goin' to the valley . . . to die."

Lone's teeth flashed in a grim smile, "He is goin' to the valley to fight. Death has been with him many years. He does not think of it." Lone's firm voice broke and shook with emotion, "Ten Bears is a great warrior.

He knows no fear. But today he will meet another great warrior, a privilege that comes to few men. They will know . . . when they face each other, Ten Bears and Josey Wales . . . and they will know their hatreds and their loves . . . but they will also know their brotherhood of courage, that the man of littleness will never know." Lone's voice had risen in an exultant thrill that was primitive and savage despite his carefully chosen words.

A thin hint of light touched the rim of the eastern canyon and silhouetted the Comanche warriors, slumped on their horses, dotting the light's edge above the ranch house. It was in this light that Josey Wales brought the big roan, frisking and prancing, to the rear of the house.

A sob tore from the throat of Laura Lee, and she rushed to the door. Lone caught and held her briefly. "He'll not like it, if ye cry," he whispered. She wiped her eyes and only stumbled once as she walked to the horse. She placed her hand on his leg, not trusting herself to speak, and looked up at him there in the saddle.

Slowly he placed his hand over hers, and the merest gleam of humor softened the hard black eyes. "Yore'er the purtiest gal in Texas, Laura Lee," he said softly, "iff'n Texas gits a queen, ye'll be it . . . fer ye fit the land . . . liken a good gun handle to a hand . . . 'er a hoss that's bred right. Ye re'clect what I'm sayin' now and mind it . . . fer it's true."

Tears welled up in her eyes, and she could not speak, and so she turned away, stumbling to the porch. Lone stood by the saddle and stretched his hand up to grasp Josey's. The grip was hard . . . the grip of brothers. He was stripped to the waist, and the wrinkled, bronze face had two streaks of white 'dobe across the cheeks and another on his forehead. It was the death face of the Cherokee . . . neither giving nor asking quarter of the enemy.

"We'll make it," Lone said to Josey, "but iff'n . . . it's otherwise . . . no women will live."

Josey nodded but didn't speak. He turned his horse away, toward the trail. As he passed, Little Moonlight touched his booted foot with the scalping knife . . . the tribute of the Cheyenne squaw, paid only to the mightiest warriors who go to their death.

As he passed from the yard, Grandma Sarah shouted . . . and her voice was clear and ringing, "Lord'll ride with ye, Josey Wales!" But if he heard, he didn't acknowledge the call . . . for he neither turned his head nor lifted his hand in farewell. The tears coursed unmindful down the withered face of Grandma Sarah, "I don't keer what they say 'bout 'em . . . reckin to me, he's twelve foot tall." She threw her apron over her face and turned back into the kitchen.

Laura Lee ran to the edge of the yard and watched him . . . the roan, held in check, stepping high and skittish as Josey Wales rode slowly down the valley by the creek and finally disappeared around the cleft of a protruding butte.

20

Ten Bears woke in his tepee at dawn and kicked the naked, voluptuous young squaw from beneath his blankets. She was lazy. His other five women already had the fire going beneath the pot. Three of them were heavy with child. He hoped the newborn would be males . . . but secretly, he knew they would come too late to follow Ten Bears. They would grow and ride and fight in the legend of Ten Bears; but Ten Bears would be dead . . . fallen in battle. This he knew.

The only two sons he had possessed were dead at the hands of the bluecoats; one of them shot cowardly under the white talking flag that the bluecoats used. Ten Bears thought of this each morning. He brooded upon it and so rekindled the hatred and vengeance

that the drug of sleep had softened in his mind . . .
and in his heart.

The bitterness rose in his throat, and he could taste
it in his mouth. Everything he loved . . . the free land
. . . his sons . . . his womenfolk . . . all had been violated
by the white man . . . most especially the bluecoat. He
savagely tore at the meat with his teeth and swallowed
big chunks in anger. Even the buffalo; once he had
ridden onto a high plain, and as far as his eye could
see lay the rotting, putrid carcasses of buffalo; killed
by the white man; not for food, not for robes, but for
some savage ceremony the white man called "sport."

Ten Bears rose and wiped the grease from his hands
on his buckskin trousers. He reached two fingers into
a pot and streaked the blue downward across his
cheeks and across his forehead; the death face of the
Comanche.

Now they would go to the white man's lodge. He
wanted them alive, if possible; so that he could slowly
burn the color from their eyes and make them scream
their cowardice; so that he could strip the skin from
their bodies and from their groins where life sprung
from the male. The womenfolk would be turned over
to the warriors . . . all of them . . . to be violated; and
if they lived, they would be given to the ones who had
captured them. The children . . . they would know that
it was Ten Bears' wrath.

Shouts came from his warriors. They had leaped to
their horses and were pointing up the valley. Ten
Bears waved for his white horse, and as a squaw
brought it forward, he sprang easily on its back and
walked him to the center of the valley, before the gathering of chiefs and braves. The sun had broken over the
eastern canyon rim and Ten Bears shaded his eyes.
The moving figure was a horseman a mile away.

He came slowly, and Ten Bears moved out to meet him. Behind Ten Bears came the chiefs, their big war bonnets setting them apart; and behind the chiefs, strung out in a line that almost crossed the valley, rode over two hundred warriors.

Ten Bears wore no bonnet . . . only a single feather. He disdained the showy headdress. But there was no mistaking him; naked from the waist up, his rifle balanced across his big white horse, he rode ten paces ahead of his chiefs, and his bearing was of one born to command.

The many horses of the Comanches made an ominous hissing sound as they paced through the long grass, carrying the half-naked riders with hideously painted faces. Behind, from the tepees, a low, ominous war drum began its beat of death. Ten Bears checked the canyon rims as he rode, and saw his scouts coming back, flanking the course of the lone rider. They signaled . . . there was only one coming to meet him.

Now the eager hate in Ten Bears was tempered with puzzlement. The man did not carry the hated white flag, and yet he came on, casually, as though he rode without care . . . but Ten Bears noticed he kept the big horse headed directly toward his white one.

Less than a hundred yards now . . . and the horse! Fit for a Chief . . . taller, more powerful than his own white charger; it almost reared as it stepped high with power, nostrils flared at the excitement. Now he could see the man. There was no rifle, but Ten Bears saw the butts of many pistols holstered on the saddle, and that the man wore three pistols. A fighting man.

He wore the hat of the Gray Riders, and what Ten Bears had at first thought . . . with a shock . . . was war paint, became a great scar on the cheek as he came closer. Almost to a collision, he came so close, so that Ten Bears was the first to stop, and the big roan reared . . . and a murmur of approval for the horse ran through the ranks of Comanche braves.

Ten Bears looked into black eyes as hard and ruthless as his own. A shivering thrill of anticipation ran through the Chief's body . . . of combat with a great warrior to match his own mettle! The rider slid a long knife from his boot, and the chiefs behind Ten Bears moved forward with a low, threatening rumble. The rider appeared not to notice as he meticulously cut a big chunk of tobacco from a twist and shoved it into his mouth. Ten Bears had not flickered an eyelash, but there was a faint glint of admiration for the audacity of a bold warrior.

"Ye'll be Ten Bears," Josey drawled and spat tobacco juice between the legs of the white horse. He had not called him "Chief" . . . nor had he called him "great," as did all the bluecoats with whom Ten Bears had talked. There was the slightest touch of casual insult . . . but Ten Bears understood. It was the way of the warrior, not the double-tongues.

"I am Ten Bears," he said slowly.

"I'm Josey Wales," Josey said. The mind of Ten Bears raced back in search of the name . . . and he knew.

"You are of the Gray Riders and you will not make peace with the bluecoats. I have heard." Ten Bears half turned on his horse and waved his arm. The chiefs and braves behind him parted, leaving an open corridor.

"You may go in peace," he said. It was a magnificent gesture befitting a great Chief, and Ten Bears was proud of the majesty it afforded him. But Josey Wales made no motion to accept this grant of life.

"I reckin not," he drawled, "I wa'ant aimin' to leave nohow. Got nowheres to go."

The horses of the Comanche braves drew closer at his refusal. Ten Bears' voice shook with anger. "Then you will die."

"I reckin," Josey said, "I come here to die with ye, or live with ye. Dyin' ain't hard fer sich as ye and me, it's the livin' thet's hard." He paused to let the words carry their weight with Ten Bears . . . then he continued, "What ye and me cares about has been butchered . . . raped. It's been done by them lyin', double-tongued snakes thet run guv'mints. Guv'mints lie . . . promise . . . back-stab . . . eat in yore lodge and rape yore women and kill when ye sleep on their promises. Guv'mints don't live together . . . men live together. From guv'mints ye cain't git a fair word . . . ner a fair fight. I come to give ye either one . . . 'er to git either one from ye."

Ten Bears straightened on his horse. The vicious hatred of Josey Wales matched his own . . . hatred for those who had killed what each of them loved. He waited, without speaking, for the outlaw to continue.

"Back there," Josey jerked his thumb over his shoulder, "is my brother, an Indian who rode with the Gray Riders, and a Cheyenne squaw, who also is my kin. There's a old squaw and a young squaw thet belongs to me. Thet's all . . . but they're liken to me . . . iff'n it's worth fightin' about, it's worth dyin' about . . . 'er don't fight. They'll fight and die. I didn't come here under no lyin' white flag to git out from under yore killin'. I come here this way, so's ye'll know that my word of death is true . . . and thet my word of life . . . then, is true."

Josey slowly waved his hand across the valley, "The

bear lives here . . . with the Comanche; the wolf, the birds, the antelope . . . the coyote. So will we live. The iron stick won't dig the ground . . . thet is my word. The game will not be killed fer sport . . . only what we eat . . . as the Comanche does. Every spring, when the grass comes, and the Comanche rides north, he can rest here in peace, and butcher cattle and jerk beef fer his travel north . . . and when the grass of the north turns brown, the Comanche can do the same, as he goes to the land of the Mexicano. The sign of the Comanche," Josey moved his hand through the air, in the wiggling sign of the snake, "will be on all the cattle. It'll be placed on my lodge, and marked on trees and on horses. Thet's my word of life."

"And your word of death?" Ten Bears asked low and threatening.

"In my pistols," Josey said, "and in yer rifles . . . I'm here fer one or t'other," and he shrugged his shoulders.

"These things you say we will have," Ten Bears said, "we already have."

"Thet's right," Josey said, "I ain't promisin' nothin' extry . . . 'ceptin' givin' ye life and ye givin' me life. I'm sayin' men can live without butcherin' one 'nother and takin' more'n what's needin' fer livin' . . . share and share alike. Reckin it ain't much to talk trade about . . . but I ain't one fer big talk . . . ner big promises."

Ten Bears looked steadily into the burning eyes of Josey Wales. The horses stomped impatiently and snorted, and along the line of warriors a ripple of anticipation marked their movements as they sensed the ending of the talk.

Slowly Josey raised the reins of his horse and placed them in his teeth. Ten Bears watched the gesture with an implacable face, but admiration came to his heart.

It was the way of the Comanche warrior . . . true and sure. Josey Wales would talk no more.

Ten Bears spoke, "It is sad that governments are chiefed by the double-tongues. There is iron in your words of death for all the Comanche to see . . . and so there is iron in your word of life. No signed paper can hold the iron, it must come from men. The word of Ten Bears, all know, carries the same iron of death . . . and of life. It is good that warriors such as we meet in the struggle of death . . . or of life. It shall be life."

Ten Bears pulled a scalping knife from his belt and slashed the palm of his right hand. He held it high for all his chiefs and braves to see, as the blood coursed down his naked arm. Josey slid the knife from his boot and slashed across his own hand. They came close and placed their hands flat and palms together and held them high.

"So it will be," said Ten Bears.

"Kin, I reckin," said Josey Wales.

Ten Bears turned his horse back through the line of braves, and they followed him slowly down the valley toward the tepees. And the drums of death stopped, and out of the hush that followed, a male thrush sent his trilling call of life across the valley.

It was Lone who saw him coming, as he first appeared around the butte and walked the roan up the trail, nearly a mile away. It was Laura Lee who could not wait. She ran from the yard, down the trail, her blond hair streaming out behind her in the wind. Grandma Sarah, Little Moonlight, and Lone stood under the cottonwood tree and watched them as Josey held his arms wide and lifted Laura Lee to the saddle before him. As they came closer, Grandma Sarah could see, through watering eyes, that Josey held

Laura Lee in his arms and that both her arms were
about his neck and her head lay on his breast.

Grandma Sarah's emotion could hold no bounds,
and so she turned on Lone and snapped, "Now ye can
warsh that heathern paint off'n yer face."

With one swoop, Lone swept Grandma Sarah from
the ground and tossed her high in the air . . . and he
laughed and shouted while Little Moonlight danced
around them and whooped. Grandma Sarah yelled
and fussed . . . but she was pleased, for when Lone set
her down, she gave him a playful slap, straightened
her skirts, and bustled into the kitchen. As Josey and
Laura Lee rode into the yard, they all could hear it
through the kitchen window; Grandma Sarah fixin'
dinner . . . and a cracked voice singing: "In the sweet
bye and bye . . ."

It was around the dinner table they talked of it. The
brand would be the Crooked River Brand; the irons
would be made by Lone, in the shape of Comanche
sign.

"It'll cost ye a hunnerd head of beef every spring,"
Josey told Grandma Sarah, "and a hunnerd every fall,
fer the Comanches of Ten Bears . . . so's we keep our
word. But I figger three, maybe four thousand head
in the valley . . . ye can still send a couple thousand
up the trail ev'ry year, to keep yer grass balanced out."

"Fair 'nough," Grandma Sarah said, "iff'n it was five
hunnerd a year . . . fair's fair. A word to share is a
word to care."

"I'll have to git riders fer the brandin'," Josey said.

Lone studied the old map, "Santo Rio, to the south,
is the closest town."

"Then I'll leave in the mornin'," Josey said.

Laura Lee came to him in his room that night, pale
in the moon that made crosses of light through the

windows and on the floor. She watched him lying there, for a long time, and seeing him awake, she whispered, "Did ye . . . did ye mean what ye said . . . about me being . . . like ye said?"

"I meant it, Laura Lee," Josey answered. She came to his bed, and after a long time she slept . . . but Josey Wales did not sleep. Deep inside, a faint hope had been born. It persisted with a promise of life . . . a rebirth he never believed could have been. In the cold light of dawn he was brought back to the reality of his position, but still, the hope was real . . . and before he left for Santo Rio, he kissed Laura Lee, secretly and long.

He rode down the valley, and the Comanche was gone; but staked at the mouth of the valley was a lance, and on it were the three feathers of peace . . . the iron word of Ten Bears. As he passed out of the valley's opening and headed south, he thought that if it could be . . . the life in this valley with Laura Lee . . . with Lone . . . with his kin . . . it would be the bloody hand of Ten Bears that gave it; the brutal, savage Ten Bears. But who could say what a savage was . . . maybe the double-tongues with their smooth manners and sly ways were the savages after all.

PART 4

21

Kelly, the bartender, swatted bottle flies in the Lost Lady saloon. Sweat dripped from the end of his nose and down his pock-marked face. He cursed the stifling noontime heat; the blazing sun that blinded the eye outside the bat wings at the door . . . and the monotony of it all.

Ten Spot, frayed cuffs and pencil-dandy mustache, dealt five-card stud at the corner table, his only customers a rundown cowboy and a seedy Mex vaquero.

"Possible straight," Ten Spot monotoned as the cards slapped.

"Nickel ante," Kelly sneered under his breath and splattered a bottle-green fly lit on the bar.

"Goddamned tinhorn," he muttered loud enough for Ten Spot to hear . . . but the gambler didn't look up. Kelly had seen REAL gamblers in New Orleans . . . before he had to leave.

Rose came out of a bedroom at the back, yawning and snatching a comb through bed-frowzed hair.

"To hell with it," she said and tossed the comb on a table. She rapped the bar, and Kelly slid a glass and bottle of Red Dog expertly to her hand.

"How much'd he have?" Kelly asked.

Rose disdained the glass and took a huge swallow from the bottle. She shuddered. "Two dollars, twenty cents," and she slapped the money on the bar. Her eyes held the hard, shiny look of women fresh from the love bed, and her mouth was smeared and mottled.

"Crap," Kelly said as he retrieved the money and spat on the floor.

Rose poured a three-finger drink in the glass to sip more leisurely. "Well," she drawled philosophically, "I ain't a young heifer no more. I might ought to paid him." She looked dreamily at the bottles behind the bar. She wasn't . . . young, that is. Her hair was supposed to be red; the label on the bottle had proclaimed that desired result . . . but it was orange where it was not streaked with gray. Her face sagged from the years and sin, and her huge breasts were hung precariously in a mammoth halter. There was no competition in Santo Rio. The last stop for Rose.

Rose was like Santo Rio, dying in the sun; used only by desperate men or lost pilgrims stumbling quickly through; refugees from places they couldn't go back to . . . watching the clock tick away the time. The end of the line; a good horse jump over Texas ground to the Rio Grande.

Josey walked the roan past the Majestic Hotel, pre-

sumptuous in the name of a faded sign; a one-story
'dobe with a sagging wooden porch. There was a horse
hitched in front, and he ran his eyes over its lines and
its rigging. The sorrel was too good for the average
cowboy, the lines too clean . . . legs too long. The
rigging was light. There were only two other horses in
town, and they stood, tails whipped between their legs
by the wind, hitch-racked before the Lost Lady saloon.

He passed the General Merchandise store and slip-
knotted the reins of the roan on the hitch rail beside
the two horses. They were cow ponies, rigged with
roping saddles. Nobody showed on the street. Santo
Rio was a night town, if anything; a border town
where the gentry did their moving by night.

When Josey Wales stepped into the Lost Lady, Rose
moved instinctively farther back along the bar. She
had seen Bill Longley and Jim Taylor, once, at Bryan,
Texas . . . but they looked tame beside this'un. A lobo.
Tied-down .44's and he stepped too quickly out of the
door's sunlight behind him, scanned the room, then
walked directly by Rose to a place at the bar's end, so
that the room and door were in his line of vision.

Hat low as he passed, hard black eyes that briefly
caught Rose with a flat look . . . and thunder! . . . that
scar, brutal and deep across the cheek. Rose felt the
hair on her neck rise stiff and tingly. The cowboy and
the vaquero twisted in their chairs to watch him, then
hastily turned back to their cards as Josey took his
place.

Kelly signified his tolerance of all humanity by placing both hands on the bar. Ten Spot appeared not to
notice . . . he was dealing.

"Whiskey?" Kelly asked.

"Beer, I reckin," Josey said casually, and Kelly drew

the beer, dark and foaming, and placed the schooner before him. Josey laid down a double eagle, and Kelly picked it up and turned it in his hand.

"The beer ain't but a nickel," he said apologetically.

"Well," Josey drawled, "reckin ye can give the boys at the table a couple bottles o' thet pizen . . . the lady here might want somethin', and have one ye'self."

"Well, now," Kelly's face brightened, "mighty decent of you, mister." The feller was high roller . . . added class, easy come, easy go . . . it was with them fellers.

"Thankee, mister," Rose murmured.

And from the card table the cowboy turned to wave a friendly thanks, and the vaquero touched his sombrero. "*Gracias, señor.*" Ten Spot flickered his eyes toward Josey and nodded.

Josey sipped the lukewarm beer, "I'm lookin' fer ropin' hands. I got a spread hunnerd miles north an' . . ."

The vaquero rose from his chair and walked to the bar. "*Señor,*" he said politely, "my *compadre,*" he indicated the cowboy who had stood up, "and myself are good with the cattle and we . . ." he laughed musically, white teeth flashing under the curling black mustache, "are a little . . . as you say, down on the luck." The vaquero extended his hand to Josey, "My name, *señor,* is Chato Olivares and this," he indicated the lean cowboy who came forward, "is *Señor* Travis Cobb."

Josey shook hands with first the vaquero and then the cowboy. "Proud t'strike up with ye," he said. He judged both of them to be in their middle forties, gray streaking the black hair of the Mexican and fading the bleached, sparse hair of the cowboy. Their clothes had seen hard wear, and their boots were heel-worn and scuffed. The faded gray eyes of Travis Cobb were inscrutable, as was the twinkling light of half humor in the black eyes of Chato.

They both wore a single pistol, sagging at the hip, but their hands were calloused from rope burns; working hands of cowboys. Josey made a snap decision.

"Fifty dollars a month and found," he said.

"Sold," drawled Travis Cobb, and his weathered face crinkled in a grin, "You could'a got me and Chato fer the found. Cain't wait to git my belly roundst some solid bunkhouse chow." He rubbed his hands in anticipation. Josey counted five double eagles on the bar.

"First month advance," he said. Chato and Travis stared unbelieving at the gold coins.

"*Hola!*" Chato breathed.

"Wal, now," Travis Cobb drawled, " 'fore I spend all of mine on sech foolishness as boots and britches, I'm a-goin' to buck the tiger agin."

Chato followed the cowboy back to the corner table . . . and Ten Spot shuffled the deck.

Kelly was in an expansive mood. He slid another schooner of beer, unasked, before Josey, and Rose moved closer to him at the bar. Kelly had noticed the scar-faced stranger had not given his name when he shook hands, but this was not unusual in Texas. It was accepted, and considered, to say the least, highly impolite to ask a gent his name.

"Well," Kelly said heartily, "rancher, huh, I'd never have thought . . ." he paused in midsentence. His eyes had strayed to a piece of paper on the shelf below the bar. He choked and his face turned red. His hands fluttered down for the paper, and he placed it on the bar.

"I ain't . . . it ain't none of my business, stranger. I

ain't never posted one of these things. Bounty hunter . . . called hisself a special deputy . . . left it in here, not an hour ago."

Josey looked down at the paper and saw himself staring back from the picture. It was a good likeness drawn by an artist's hand. The Confederate hat . . . the black eyes and mustache . . . the deep scar; all made it unmistakable. The print below the picture told his history and ended with: EXTREMELY QUICK AND ACCURATE WITH PISTOLS. WILL NOT SURRENDER. DO NOT ATTEMPT TO DISARM. WANTED DEAD: $7,500 REWARD. The name JOSEY WALES stood out in bold letters.

Rose had moved close to read. Now she edged away from the bar. Josey looked up. There was no mistaking the man who had stepped through the door. His garb was dandy leather; tall and lean-hipped; and his holster was tied low on his right leg. Josey took one look and held it steady, locked in challenge with the pale, almost colorless eyes. He was a professional pistolman . . . and he obviously knew his trade.

Josey took a half step from the bar, and his body slid into the half crouch. Rose had stumbled backward into a table, and she half leaned, half stood, in a frozen position. Kelly had his back against the bottles, and Ten Spot, Chato, and Travis Cobb were turned, motionless, in their chairs. The old Seth Thomas clock, pride of Santo Rio, ticked loud in the room. Wind whined around the corner of the building and whipped a miniature dust cycle under the bat-wing door. The bounty hunter's speech was expressionless.

"You'd be Josey Wales."

"I reckin," Josey's tone was deceptively casual.

"You're wanted, Wales," he said.

"Reckin I'm right popular," Josey's mouth twitched with sardonic humor.

The silence fell on them again. The buzzing of a fly sounded huge in the room. The bounty hunter's eyes wavered before those of Josey Wales, and Josey almost whispered, "It ain't necessary, son, ye can leave . . . and ride."

The eyes wavered more wildly, and suddenly he whirled and bolted through the bat wings into the street.

Everyone came to life at once . . . except Josey Wales. He stood in the same position, as Kelly exclaimed and Rose plumped down in a chair and wiped her face with her skirts. The moment of relief came quickly to an end. The bounty hunter stepped back into the saloon. His face was ashen, and his eyes were bitter.

"I had to come back," he said with surprising calm.

"I know," Josey said. He knew, once a pistolman was broken, he was walking dead; the nerve gone and reputation shattered. He wouldn't last past the story of his breaking, which would always go ahead of him wherever he went.

Now the bounty hunter's hand swept for his holster, sure and fluid. He was fast. He cleared leather as a .44 slug caught him low in the chest, and he hammered two shots into the floor of the saloon. His body curved in, like a flower closing for the night, and he slid slowly to the floor.

Josey Wales stood, feet wide apart, smoke curling from the barrel of the pistol in his right hand. And in that smoke, he saw with bitter acceptance . . . there would be no new life for Josey Wales.

He left him there, face down on the floor, after arranging with Ten Spot and Kelly for his burial . . . and their split of the dead man's meager wealth in payment for the task. It was the rough decency and justice of Texas.

"I'll read over him," Ten Spot promised in his cold voice, and Josey, Chato, and Travis Cobb forked their broncs north, toward the Crooked River Ranch; past the spot where the bounty hunter would be buried, nameless; but with the simple cross to mark another violent death on the wild, windy plains of West Texas.

22

Chato Olivares and Travis Cobb took to the Crooked River Ranch, as Lone said, "like wild hawgs to a swamp waller." They were good ropers and reckless riders . . . and enthusiastic eaters at Grandma Sarah's table. The two riders lived in the comfortable bunkhouse but took their meals in the kitchen of the main house with everybody else. Grandma Sarah was flustered, then pleased at the courtly, Old World manner of Chato Olivares. She thanked the Lord for it in one of her open Sunday prayer-sermons, adding that "sich manners brangs us to notice of civilization, which some othern's hereabouts might try doin'."

Josey and Lone rode with the cowboys, searching the cows out of brush-choked arroyos and back into the valley. It was hard, sweating work, rising before dawn and moving cattle until dark. They built a fan-shaped corral in one of the arroyos and narrowed down the high fencing until only a single cow could come through the chute. Here, in the chute, they slapped the Crooked River Brand of the Comanche sign to their hides and turned them loose, snorting and bawling, back into the valley.

Only yearlings and mavericks had to be roped and thrown, and Chato and Travis were experts with their long loops. They disdained "dallying"; the technique, after roping the cow, of whipping the rope in a tripping motion about the cow's legs. They were two expert, prideful workmen at their trade.

Josey lingered on through the long summer months. He knew he should have left already . . . before the men came riding for him; before those who loved him were forced into violence because of their loyalty. He silently cursed his own weakness in staying . . . but he put off the leaving . . . savoring the hard work, the lounging with the cowboys after the day's work ended; even the Sunday "services"; the peacefulness of summer Sunday afternoons, when he walked with Laura Lee on the banks of the creek and beside the waterfall. They kissed and held hands, and made love in the shadows of the willows, and Laura Lee's face shone with a happiness that bubbled in her eyes, and like all women . . . she made plans. Josey Wales grew quieter in his guilt; in his sin of staying where he should not stay. He could not tell her.

Josey gradually pushed Lone to the ramrod position of the ranch and took to riding more alone, leaving it to Lone to direct the work. He sent Travis Cobb east on a week's ride in search of border ranches for news of trail herding; where they might bunch their cattle with others . . . in the spring . . . for the drive north. Travis returned and brought good news of the Goodnight-Loving Trail through New Mexico Territory that bypassed Kansas and ended at Denver.

Once, at supper, Josey had almost told them, when Grandma Sarah abruptly proposed, before everyone, that Josey accept a fourth interest in the ranch. "It ain't nothin' but right," she had said.

Josey had looked around the table and shook his head, "I'd ruther ye give any part of mine to Lone . . . he's gittin' old . . . maybe the ol' Cherokee needs a place to set in the sun."

Little Moonlight had laughed . . . she had understood . . . and stood up at the table and boldly ran her hand over a suspiciously growing mound of her shapely belly, "Old . . . Ha!" Everybody joined in the laughter except Grandma Sarah.

"They's goin' to be some marryin' up takin' place 'round here . . . with several folks I know."

Laura Lee had blushed red and shyly looked at Josey . . . and everybody laughed again.

Late summer faded softly, and the first cool nip touched the edge of the wind, putting the early glow of gold on the cottonwood trees along the creek. Josey Wales knew the word had gone back from the border . . . from Santo Rio . . . and he knew he had stayed too long.

It was Grandma Sarah who gave him the opening. At supper she complained of the need for supplies, and Josey said, too quickly, "I'll go." And across the glow of tallow candles his eyes met Lone's. The Cherokee knew . . . but he said nothing.

He saddled up in the early morning light, and the smell of fall was on the wind. He was taking Chato with him, and two packhorses . . . but only Chato and the horses would return. Lone came to the corral and watched him cinch the saddle down and place the heavy roll . . . a roll for long travel . . . behind the cantle.

Josey turned to the Indian and pressed a bag of gold coins in his hand. He passed it off lightly, "Thet ain't none o' mine . . . got mine right here," and he patted a saddlebag, "Thet there's yore'n, it was . . . Jamie's part, so . . . it's yore'n now. He'd a'wanted it used fer . . . the folks." They gripped hands in the dim light, and the tall Cherokee didn't speak.

"Tell Little Moonlight," Josey began, ". . . ah, hell, I'll be ridin' back this way and name thet young'un ye got comin'." They both knew he wouldn't, and Lone pulled away. He stumbled on his way to the 'dobe in the cedars.

Chato was mounted and leading the packhorses out of the yard when Josey saw Laura Lee. She came from the kitchen, shy in her nightgown, and shyer still, raised her face to him. He kissed her for a long time.

"This time," she whispered in his ear, "ye tell them in town to send the first preacher man up here thet comes ridin' through."

Josey looked down at her, "I'll tell 'em, Laura Lee."

He had ridden from the yard when he stopped and turned in the saddle. She was still standing as he had left her, the long hair about her shoulders. He called out, "Laura Lee, don't fergit what I told ye . . . thet time . . . about ye being the purtiest gal in Texas."

"I won't forget," she said softly.

Far down the trail of the valley he looked back and saw her still, at the edge of the yard, and the tiny figure of Grandma Sarah was close by her. On a knoll, off to the side, he saw Lone watching . . . the old

cavalry hat on his head . . . and he thought he saw
Little Moonlight, beside him, lift her hand and wave
. . . but he couldn't be sure . . . the wind smarted his
eyes and watered his vision so that he could see none
of them anymore.

23

Josey and Chato night-camped ten miles out of Santo Rio and rode into town in late morning of the following day. Chato had been subdued on the trip, his usual good humor giving way to long periods of silence that matched Josey's. They had not spoken of Josey's leaving, but Chato knew the reputation of the outlaw and was wise in the ways of the border. The news of the Santo Rio killing could not have been kept secret . . . there was nothing for a gunfighter to do but move on. Chato dreaded the parting.

They hitched and loaded the supplies on the pack-horses in front of the General Mercantile. Meal and flour, sugar and coffee, bacon and beans . . . sacksful of fancies. As they filled the last sack to be strapped on the horse, Josey placed a lady's yellow straw hat with flowing ribbon on top. He looked across the horse's

back at Chato, "It's fer Laura Lee. Ye tell her . . ." he
let the sentence die.

Chato looked at the ground, "I understand, *señor*,"
he mumbled, "I shall tell her."

"Well," Josey said with an air of finality, "let's git a
drink."

They left their horses before the store and walked to
the Lost Lady. He would have the drink with Chato,
and Chato would head north with the packhorses,
back to the ranch. Josey Wales would cross the Rio
Grande.

Ten Spot was playing solitaire at the corner table
when they came in. Josey and Chato walked past two
men at the bar having drinks and took up their places
at the end. Rose was seated at a table, alone, and she
cast a warning glance at Josey as he tossed her a greet-
ing, "Mornin', Miss Rose . . .," and was instantly on his
guard.

The atmosphere was strained and tense. Kelly
brought the beer to them, but his face was white and
drawn. He mopped the bar vigorously in front of
Chato and Josey and under his breath he whispered,
"Pinkerton man, and something called a Texas Ranger
. . . lookin' for you." Chato stiffened and his smile
faded. Josey lifted the schooner of beer to his lips, and
over the rim he studied the two men.

They were talking together in low tones. Both were
big men, but where the one wore a derby hat and
Eastern suit, the other wore a battered cowboy hat
that proved the quality of Mr. Stetson's work. His face
was weathered by the wind, and his clothes were the
garb of any cowboy. They both wore pistols on their
hips, and a sawed-off shotgun was lying before them
on the bar. They were professional policemen, though
from two separate worlds.

Kelly was flicking specks from the bar, finding here-tofore unseen spots and industriously rubbing the bar cloth at them. He was between the outlaw at one end of the bar and the lawmen at the other. Kelly didn't like his position. Now he scowled with a bleary look at a spot near Josey and attacked it with the cloth.

"Pinkerton man's federal," he whispered to Josey, "cowboy feller is Texas . . . fer Gawd's sake, man!" and he moved away, back up the bar, flicking dust from bottles. Chato slid a quick look at Josey as he sipped his beer. The men stopped their low talk and now looked down the bar, frankly and openly, at Josey and Chato.

The Ranger spoke into the heavy silence, and his tone was calm and drawling, "We're law officers, and we're looking for Josey Wales." There was no hint of fear in either of the lawmen's faces.

Chato, on Josey's left, stepped carefully away from the bar, and his tone was thinly polite, "The shotgun, *señores,* stays on the bar."

Josey didn't take his eyes from the men, but to Chato, in a voice that carried over the room, he said, "T'ain't yore call, Chato. Ye're paid to ride . . . reckin thet's what ye'd better be doin'."

The polite voice of Chato answered him, *"No comprendo.* I ride . . . and fight, for the brand. It is my honor, *señor."*

Not a breath was drawn, not a hand moved, except Ten Spot, who dealt his solitaire, seemingly oblivious of it all. Ten Spot laid a black eight on a black nine . . . it was the only way to beat the hand. From the corner table, his voice was thin and casual, as though remarking on the weather, "I seen Josey Wales shot down in Monterrey, seven . . . maybe eight weeks ago.

Me and Rose was takin' a little *paseo* down that way
. . . seen him take on five pistoleros. He got three of
'em before they cut him down. Ask Rose."

For the first time since he began speaking, Ten Spot
looked up and addressed himself to Josey, "I was in-
tending to tell you about it, Mr. Wells . . . next time
you came in. It was a real hoolihan . . ." and then to
the lawmen, "This is Mr. Wells, a rancher north of
here." Ten Spot broke the deck and started a new
shuffle.

Rose's voice was high and squeaky, "I was goin' to
tell you 'bout it, Mr. Wells, you remember, last time
you was in here, we was . . . uh, discussing that outlaw."

Behind the bar Kelly was nodding vigorously with
encouragement to the speakers. Neither Josey nor
Chato spoke . . . nor did they move. The lawmen
talked in low tones to each other. The Ranger looked
at Ten Spot, "Will you sign an affidavit to that?" he
asked.

"Yep," Ten Spot said and laid a red deuce on a red
trey.

"And you, Miss . . . er . . . Rose?" the Ranger looked
at Rose.

"Why shore," Rose said, "whatever that is," and she
took a healthy slug from a bottle of Red Dog.

The Pinkerton man took paper and pencil from his
coat and wrote vigorously at the bar.

"Here," he said and handed the pencil to Ten Spot,
who came forward and signed his name. The Pinkerton man looked at the signature and frowned, "Your
name is . . . Wilbur Beauregard Francis Willingham?"
he asked incredulously.

Ten Spot drew himself up to full height in his tattered frock coat. "It is, suh," he said stiffly, "of the Virginia Willinghams. I trust the name does not offend you, suh."

"Oh, no offense, no offense," the Pinkerton man said hastily.

Ten Spot, formally and stiffly, inclined his body in a slight bow. Rose took the pencil and brushed imaginary dust from the paper, hesitated, and brushed again, while her face reddened.

"The lady," Ten Spot said brusquely, "broke her reading glasses, unfortunately, while we were in Monterrey. Under the circumstances, if you will accept a simple mark from her, I will witness her signature."

"We'll accept it," the Ranger said dryly.

Rose laboriously made her mark and walked with whiskey dignity back to her table.

The Pinkerton man looked at the paper, folded it, and stuck it in his breast pocket. "Well . . ." he said uncertainly to the Ranger, "I guess that's it."

The Texas Ranger looked at the ceiling with a calculating eye, like he was counting the roof poles. "I reckon," he said, "there's about five thousand wanted men this year, in Texas. Cain't git 'em all . . . ner would want to. We jest come out of a War, and they's bound to be tore-up ground . . . and men . . . where a herd's stampeded. Way I figger it, what's GOOD, depends on whose a-sayin' it. What's good back east where them politicians is at . . . might not be good fer Texas. Texas is a-goin' to git straightened out . . . it'll take good men . . . Texas style o' good . . . meaning tough and straight . . . to do it. Takes iron to beat iron." He sighed as he turned toward the door, thinking of the long, dusty ride ahead.

"If yore're comin' back this way, stop in," Kelly invited.

The Ranger looked meaningfully, not at Kelly, but at Josey Wales. "Reckon we won't be back," he said, and with a wave of his hand he was gone.

For the first time in nine years Josey Wales was stunned. Where a moment before, his future was the grim, tedious trail of outlawry . . . of leaving those he had come to love . . . the valley he had so bitterly left behind; now it was life, a new life, that staggered his thinking and his emotions. Done, here in a saloon; in a run-down, sour-smelling saloon by people no one would look twice at on the streets of the cities; by men, among men . . . as Ten Bears had said.

Chato laughed and slapped him on the back. Kelly, completely contrary to his practice, set up the house. Ten Spot, thin smile and dead eyes, was shaking his hand, and Rose propped a heavy breast on his shoulder and kissed him enthusiastically.

Josey walked to the door, followed by the jingling spurs of Chato . . . like a man in a dream. He paused and looked back at these who would be judged as derelicts by those wont to judge. "My friends," he said, "when ye can find a preacher, bring 'em to the ranch. Miss Rose, ye'll stand up with my bride, and Ten Spot, ye and Kelly will stand with me. Ye'll come, 'er me and Chato will come and git ye."

Ten Spot, Rose, and Kelly watched from the saloon door as the two riders headed north. Suddenly they saw the riders spur their mounts. They whipped their pistols from holsters and shot into the air . . . and floating back came the wild yells of exuberant Texans . . . exuberance . . . and a lust for life.

"We'll git the padre from across the river," Kelly shouted. But the outlaw and the vaquero were too far away . . . and too noisy to hear.

Ten Spot slipped a sidelong glance at Rose, "I'll buy you a drink, Rose," he invited . . . and at her lifted eyebrow, he smiled, "No obligation . . . this one is for Texas."

24

They came a week later; Ten Spot, Rose, and Kelly. They brought the padre; a fiddlin' man; two extra vaqueros, one of whom brought his guitar; and three sloe-eyed *señoritas*, who had come "good timin'" across the river. They came loaded down with Texas gifts, like a pair of boots for Laura Lee, bottles of red-eye, kegs of beer, and a ribbon for Grandma Sarah's hair. They came ready . . . rootin', tootin', Texas-style . . . for a wedding, and got two of them; Josey and Laura Lee, Lone and Little Moonlight.

Rose was resplendent as Maid of Honor in a sequined gold dress with tassels that shimmied as she walked. The padre frowned briefly at Little Moonlight's stomach, but he sighed and resigned himself; it was the way of Texas. Little Moonlight enjoyed the white man's ceremony immensely, and as instructed, shouted "Shore!" when asked to be Lone's wife.

The celebration lasted a number of days, in Texas tradition, until the fiddler's hands were too stiff to pull the bow . . . and the liquor ran out.

The wedding wasn't decently over and gone, before an almond-eyed girl was born to Little Moonlight . . . and Lone. Grandma Sarah fussed over the baby and rendered sermon-prayers to Laura Lee and Josey that sich was pleasing to the eyes of God.

The falls and the springs came, and Ten Bears rested and made medicine with his people, in their way. Until the autumn when Ten Bears and the Comanche came no more. The word of iron had been true. And Josey thought of it . . . what might have been . . . if men like the Ranger could have settled with Ten Bears . . . as he had. The thought came back mostly in the haunting, smoky haze of Indian Summer . . . each fall, when the gold and red touched the valley, in remembrance of the Comanche.

The firstborn to Josey and Laura Lee was a boy; blue-eyed and blond, and now Grandma Sarah relaxed to grow old in the contentment that the seed was replenished in the land. They did not name the baby boy after his father; Josey Wales insisted. And so they called him Jamie.